April's Hand Trembled And Gripped The Covers Tighter. "Why Wouldn't I Remember? Did I Hurt My Head?"

Seth stilled as he studied April's face for signs of duplicity. Somehow she'd bamboozled his brother Jesse into swapping the Lighthouse Hotel for a next-to-worthless recording studio and label. And now that Jesse was dead and Seth had come to fix the situation, she was claiming amnesia.

Seth didn't believe in coincidence, and something about her memory loss seemed far too… convenient.

He refocused on the heartbreakingly beautiful woman lying in the hospital bed. Her lips trembled; her eyes were huge in her delicate face. The overall effect was alluring and deceptively vulnerable. He crossed his arms over his chest.

He couldn't afford to be swayed.

Dear Reader,

When I was young, like many kids, I had piano lessons. Unfortunately for my teacher and those who had to listen to me practice, I had neither talent nor any semblance of hand-eye coordination. But boy, I wanted to be able to play well. So it was natural to give the ability to one of my heroines and live vicariously through her. April can play the way I wish I could and, like a true hero, Seth admires that about her. All my childhood dreams coming to life.

This is the second story in three connected books about half brothers (though it stands alone, too). *At the Billionaire's Beck and Call?* had Ryder Bramson's story, and after Seth will come the third brother, JT Hartley. While writing Ryder's book, there was no doubt he was my favorite hero to date, but once I started *Million-Dollar Amnesia Scandal,* I have to admit, Seth quickly stole my heart. So honorable, so focused, so gorgeous. He needed a special heroine.

April is struggling with amnesia through this story, and starts to wonder if she'll ever get her memory back and what that would mean for her identity. I found those concepts fascinating—if *you* lost all your memories, would you be the same person? Make the same decisions?

I hope you enjoy April and Seth's story as much as I enjoyed writing it. And if you want some extra "behind the scenes" tidbits, visit me at www.rachelbailey.com.

Rachel

RACHEL BAILEY

MILLION-DOLLAR
AMNESIA SCANDAL

Published by Silhouette Books
America's Publisher of Contemporary Romance

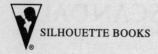

SILHOUETTE BOOKS

ISBN-13: 978-0-373-73083-4

Recycling programs
for this product may
not exist in your area.

MILLION-DOLLAR AMNESIA SCANDAL

Books by Rachel Bailey

Silhouette Desire

Claiming His Bought Bride #1992
The Blackmailed Bride's Secret Child #1998
At the Billionaire's Beck and Call? #2039
Million-Dollar Amnesia Scandal #2070

RACHEL BAILEY

developed a serious book addiction at a young age (via Peter Rabbit and Jemima Puddleduck) and has never recovered. Just how she likes it. She went on to earn degrees in psychology and social work, but is now living her dream—writing romance for a living.

She lives on a piece of paradise on Australia's Sunshine Coast with her hero and four dogs, where she loves to sit with a dog or two, overlooking the trees and reading books from her ever-growing to-be-read pile.

Rachel would love to hear from you and can be contacted through her website, www.rachelbailey.com.

For Jody,
who plaited my hair when I was little,
who gets all my obsessions and shares them, and who
always believed my writing was good, even when it wasn't.
A more fabulous eldest sister would be hard to imagine.

Acknowledgments

Charles Griemsman and Shana Smith for their editing of
this book, and Jenn Schober for her support.

Robyn Grady, Barb JG and Sharon Archer for
reading early drafts and their invaluable suggestions.

John, who makes writing possible.

One

As he looked around the private New York hospital room, Seth Kentrell dug his hands deep into his pockets. The best medical treatment money could buy, delivered in a room that wouldn't look out of place in one of his own high-end hotels. For someone like the world-renowned jazz singer, April Fairchild, he wouldn't expect anything less.

He glanced over at the woman lying seemingly unscathed in the hospital bed, her eyes closed, her delicate skin pale... and more sublimely fascinating than he'd expected. Her image was familiar, but in the flesh, she was exquisite. Even in sleep.

Was that what his brother had thought—had she taken Jesse to her bed? Was that how she'd manipulated him into practically giving her one of the prized hotels from their portfolio? At the thought of his brother, a sledgehammer blow hit the center of his chest. It'd been eight days and it was still beyond belief that Jesse was gone. Dead. Seth clenched his fists tight in his pockets, as if that could relieve the ache. But nothing could take the crushing sense of loss away. He'd never see his brother again.

And this woman had been the last person to see Jesse alive.

As he took a step closer, she moved restlessly in her sleep and he paused, not wanting to wake her. He had no idea of the true extent of the injuries she'd sustained in the accident that had killed his brother—the media had been fed meaningless and general information only. Which was why he'd had to come.

April moved again, and her face pinched then relaxed. Seth frowned. Was she in pain? Were there bruises marring her loveliness under the covers? He sucked in a breath, wondering if he should call a nurse. What if—

He stopped himself midthought and scrubbed his hands through his hair. He couldn't let himself lose track of why he'd come. He needed the Lighthouse Hotel back or he risked losing the alliances he'd carefully built on the board of directors. By leaving equal shares in the conglomerate to his legitimate and illegitimate families, his father's will had tried to bring his sons together but had instead thrown down the gauntlet. With Jesse's death, the shares he and Seth had jointly inherited had reverted to Seth, but that just meant he and his half brother, Ryder Bramson, now had an equal half each of Warner's stock. And now another man, JT Hartley, had emerged, claiming to be a long-lost son of Warner, demanding a share of the will. Though he wouldn't get that far—Seth would make sure of it.

Likewise Seth had no intention of losing to Ryder Bramson. In the space of mere months, he'd lost his father and Jesse; he wouldn't lose his company as well—no matter how lovely or vulnerable April Fairchild seemed to be.

The door opened and closed behind him and he pivoted

to see a middle-aged, overly thin woman step purposefully into the room.

She snagged him with her gaze. "Are you another doctor?" she asked with the air of someone in charge.

"No."

"A physiotherapist?"

"I'm not with the hospital."

Her spine stiffened. "Are you a reporter?"

"No. My name is Seth Kentrell."

Her eyes widened as she recognized the name. "How did you get in?"

A reasonable question. He'd told April's guard at the door that he was from her lawyer's office and showed him her name on the contract he held. The man had at least checked the name, but it had been too easy to pass. Had he been on the Bramson Holdings' security staff, Seth would have him fired.

But he wasn't here to share details about security.

He arched an eyebrow. "The question you should be asking is why I'm here."

"You're the intruder. I'll ask the questions." She bit on her lip, clearly wanting to ask precisely what he'd suggested, but now reluctant. Then she gave in. "Why are you here?"

He rewarded her with a smile. "To save Ms. Fairchild from a nasty, very public legal battle. Believe me, it's in her best interests to talk to me sooner rather than later."

Small noises came from the bed, and he turned to see April waking, her lashes blinking against the light, then opening to reveal large, chestnut-brown eyes. Her gaze fixed on him and the breath caught in his lungs. She was like a crushed rose, forlorn and broken, yet still exquisitely beautiful. Her fair skin was as perfect as porcelain; her hair—a tumble of caramel and honey—sat about her shoulders. He had the strange sensation of being drawn closer, closer. But, no, he tore his gaze away and steadied himself.

Shoulders squared, he looked back to April. She was squinting to see; there was too much light in the room. He crossed to the windows and drew the drapes closed, and she relaxed a fraction, opening her eyes more fully.

The older woman rushed over and sat on the edge of the bed. "April, darling, you're awake."

April frowned, then winced as if frowning hurt. "I think you've made a mistake," she rasped.

Seth raised an eyebrow. "You seem awake. Hard to mistake that."

She looked back to him, and shook her head very slowly. "My name's not April."

The woman gripped April's hand and spoke gently, as if to a slow child. "Yes it is. April Fairchild. My daughter."

So this was the mother. And her daughter's manager, according to his research. Seth ran an appraising glance over her. She reminded him of a spider, with her sticklike arms and legs, and the way she was watching April, as if waiting for her daughter to come deeper into her web. Every instinct told him not to trust spiderwoman. But the bigger issue was why she was telling April what her own name was. He rocked back on his heels, waiting for their next move.

April sat up a little and looked intently at her mother, then lay back on the pillow. "I'm sorry, but I don't know you. You've made some kind of mistake."

The woman smiled tightly. "Tell me about your mother then. And your name."

April's warm brown eyes flew from her mother to him and back again, panic starting to fill their depths.

The woman leaned over and cupped her cheek. "Don't worry, darling, the doctors said you'll remember soon."

"Remember soon?" Seth was all attention.

April laid a pale hand over her chest, gripping the covers. "How long have I been here?"

"Eight days," her mother said, giving the same tight smile. "You were unconscious for the first five, but you've been waking up for the last three, and each time you don't remember."

April's hand trembled and gripped the covers tighter. "Why wouldn't I remember? Did I hurt my head?"

"The doctors say your brain is fine," her mother said in a singsong voice, clearly forgetting to be discreet in a stranger's presence. "You have retrograde amnesia. It'll all settle down soon and you'll remember everything."

Seth stilled as he studied April's face for signs of duplicity. Somehow she'd bamboozled his brother Jesse into swapping the Lighthouse Hotel for a next-to-worthless recording studio and label. And now that Jesse was dead and he'd come to fix the situation, she was claiming amnesia.

Seth didn't believe in coincidence, and something about her memory loss seemed far too…convenient.

He refocused on the heartbreakingly beautiful woman lying in the hospital bed. Her lips trembled. Her eyes were huge in her delicate face. The overall effect was alluring and deceptively vulnerable. He crossed his arms over his chest. He couldn't afford to be swayed.

April turned back to the woman stroking her hand. "You're my mother?"

"Yes."

April looked at him, her gaze searching. "And who are you? My boyfriend?" He didn't say anything, but his pulse spiked at the thought of being her lover. She swallowed hard. "Husband?"

Her mother leaned into her line of vision, severing the connection. "You've never met him before. He shouldn't be here," she said, fidgeting with the edge of the sheet with her free hand.

Seth casually stepped to the side, a counter to the block the mother had provided. "And yet, here I am."

"I think it's time you left. We can talk about that matter when—"

"Are you sure my name's April?" She cut her mother off, anxiety again marring her features. "Surely my own name would be familiar."

Her mother forced an overly bright smile. "You're April Fairchild. I'm very sure, since I filled out your birth certificate."

April sucked in her bottom lip and rolled it between her teeth as she turned to him. "Then who are you?"

The intensity of her gaze shot through his body, heated his blood.

He cleared his throat. "Seth Kentrell. We have an urgent business matter to discuss."

"Urgent enough to come to my hospital bed?" She blinked up at him, all confused innocence, but Seth reminded himself that she was a performer. She'd been singing on stage since she was thirteen.

Her need for hospitalization after a major car accident wasn't in question. Whether she was making the most of an opportunity to gain an expensive hotel from him was another matter entirely. "Yes."

She frowned, then winced. Her hands gingerly touched her temples. "What happened to me?"

Her mother's spider fingers gripped her hand again. "You were in a car accident."

April drew in a long breath. "Do you think you could get me some aspirin?"

Seth leaned closer, careful not to jostle her, and pressed a button on the panel above her bed for the nurse. She leaned her head back into the pillow to look up at him as he did, her eyes clearly asking if he and her mother were lying to her. He paused, hand still resting on the bed head. Could she be telling the truth and really have lost her memory?

The nurse bustled in and disengaged the call button.

Regaining his equilibrium, Seth stepped back. "Ms. Fairchild needs pain medication."

The nurse picked up the chart at the end of the bed and asked April several questions, took her temperature and pulse. And all the while, April watched him. She looked lost, clinging to his gaze like a life raft. The urge to protect her inexplicably reared in his chest, and he closed his eyes for a moment against the power of it. When he opened them again, he focused on the nurse.

She wrote something on April's chart, seeming satisfied, then went to the trolley she'd brought in and shook two tablets from a bottle. "This will help with the headache. The doctor will be along in an hour or two and will answer your questions."

"Again," her mother said quietly.

On her way out the door, the nurse turned a sharp glance on April's mother and then him. "Ten more minutes, and don't upset her. She's still healing."

But—the million-dollar question—how much healing was there to do? She'd woken from the coma three days ago, plenty of time to cook up a strategy with Mommy Manager. They would want more time to counter the legal challenge to April's ownership of the Lighthouse Hotel. Surely, April had been expecting a challenge once Jesse died. Faking amnesia would certainly give her that time.

"You don't believe me, do you, Mr. Kentrell?" April's soft voice broke through his thoughts.

He cleared his throat then told her the truth. "I haven't decided yet."

"Why would I pretend?"

"To avoid dealing with me." He shrugged one shoulder as he called her bluff. "Perhaps a publicity stunt."

"Publicity? Who else would care?" She blinked slowly, her eyes large. There was intelligence behind those eyes. But was the intelligence calculating which words to use for manipulation, or was she honestly struggling to understand?

He ran through his options for playing the situation. For the moment, he needed to base his actions on the assumption she was faking. Which meant he could straight-out accuse her of lying, which would only garner him a denial. Or he could play along and wait for her to trip up.

He stalked to the window and drew back the curtains, letting sunlight flood the room once more.

"Can she walk?" he asked her mother.

"She was given clearance a few days ago when she first woke."

"Does she have any body injuries?"

The mother appeared hesitant to divulge further information, so he graced her with a practiced smile. "I'm here to help. If everyone cooperates, I'll be able to protect her from the scandal of a legal battle."

Eyes widening in alarm, Mrs. Fairchild nodded. "It was mainly bruises, and they've pretty much healed. Though her balance has been affected, and she's not supposed to get up without the physiotherapist here."

Seth nodded, then walked to April. "I'll carry you to the window. There's something I need to show you."

* * *

Carry her? April's heart raced. Everything—the room, this woman holding her hand, her explanation—was surreal, like a dream; instinctively, she knew it was really happening. The lights were too bright to be a dream, the man too alive. He was a flesh-and-blood man, no question, pulsing with vitality and heat. And when she focused on that heat in his eyes, she knew she was alive, too.

He cast her a sidelong look as he stood there all tall and dark, and for a moment she was stunned by the intensity of his eyes. On the surface, he looked like a respectable businessman; but those eyes…they were navy blue, and filled with tightly leashed emotion. There was an edge of danger to this man, an edge—she would guess—he kept carefully controlled at all times. It took her breath away.

Stomach churning, she broke away from his gaze. This situation was spinning out of control. But then, had anything felt remotely like control since she'd woken? She'd only just been able to hold at bay the panic triggered by the woman's assertion that she was her mother and her own name was April.

And now this man was suggesting he pick her up in his arms. If he was a stranger, as he said he was, she didn't want him carrying her—she already felt he was too close, his looks too intimate for someone she'd never met before. She looked down at herself through the thick hospital bedspread. Besides a monster of a headache and the anxiety filling every limb and organ, her body at least felt in working order.

"I can walk."

And then a thought struck. Was she decently dressed? She lifted the covers and found she wore a long, emerald-green nightdress that laced up the front. A nightdress was far from equal to his suit, but at least it adequately covered her from neck to ankles.

One hand pressed to her throbbing temple, she slowly swung one foot from under the covers to the floor. Seth moved to stand beside the bed, not close enough to crowd, but his presence was strangely reassuring, and she let out a breath. She slid the other foot out to join the first, wiggling her feet on the tiles to make sure they were stable, then she slowly rose from the bed.

The room slanted and spun and panic flared in her chest. She couldn't do it; she felt herself sway and knew her muscles had no hope of catching her. But before she could fall, Seth was there holding her, and without a second thought she leaned into his strong frame, gripped his shirtfront tightly as his powerful arms banded around her, supporting her trembling legs.

Dragging in choppy breaths, she didn't move. Neither did he. As if from a distance, she heard the woman claiming to be her mother asking if she was all right, but she ignored the questions. It was all she could do to let Seth hold her while she tried to steady the world again.

The room gradually stilled and she became aware of the man whose arms were about her. With her nose pressed to his chest, she breathed in his scent. It reminded her of a forest—fresh, natural, a taste of the woods on the wind. A scent that made her feel safe and at the same time gave her a sense of being fully alive.

She took a deep breath, willed her body to be strong, and centered her weight back on her own legs. "Thank you. I'll be fine to walk now."

"I don't think so." He scooped her up in one smooth motion.

Surprised, and with no other option, she wrapped her arms around his neck and held on tight. She wanted to tell him to put her down, that she didn't care what his point was anymore, she just wanted to lie back in the hospital bed. But before she could get the words out, he'd walked the few paces to the window.

He gestured with his chin. "Those people are here for you."

April looked outside. There was a huge swarm of people gathered several floors down, around what was probably the entrance to the hospital. Most had cameras around their necks, others stood near television equipment.

All those people there for her? Her stomach hollowed and a strange coldness spread across her skin.

"I'm famous?" she whispered in disbelief.

"Very." Seth said the word with a twisted smile. The look told her clearly what his words did not. He still didn't believe her.

He was a stranger to her—why should it matter what he believed? But it did. She wanted those eyes of darkest blue to look at her with acknowledgment, respect. She wanted to say the words that would make him understand what was going on in her head.

Instead, she twisted in his arms to face her mother. "Why am I famous?"

The woman's hands fluttered around her face. "Darling, I think you should go back to bed."

Arching her neck back, she repeated the question to Seth. "Why am I famous?"

He hesitated, seemed to be weighing up whether to humor her further or not. Then he relaxed a fraction. "You're a singer."

A vision flashed in her mind—sitting at a piano, singing into a microphone on a stage before thousands of people. And for a moment the panic eased. "I play the piano, too."

"Yes," he said tightly, then carried her back to bed. He laid her down with infinite care, barely causing her head to jostle.

She adjusted herself against the pillows, then looked to Seth. "Are you in the music industry?"

"No, I'm in the hotel business." He watched her sharply, as if that should mean something to her.

She suddenly knew he was very serious about why he'd come here. She just hoped they weren't opponents, because—if his eyes were telling the truth—Seth Kentrell would be a force to be reckoned with.

She sucked in a deep breath. "So tell me why you're here."

"You have one of my hotels," he said, eyes focused like a lion's on its prey. "I don't know how you got it, but I want it back."

Seth watched April frown in apparent confusion. "How could I have one of your hotels?"

"It's a good question, but at this point, irrelevant." He reached into his inside coat pocket and retrieved the folded paperwork. "You signed a contract giving you ownership, and I need you to sign these papers to rescind that contract."

Of course, if she really did have amnesia and he got her to sign the new contract under these conditions, there was a chance it could be thrown out of court. But it was better than doing nothing.

She held his gaze as she took the pages, but she didn't open them. "If I've never met you before, how have I bought your hotel? Or was it done through lawyers, and you somehow accidentally signed approval?"

No, it had been done by somehow coercing his brother and keeping the deal secret. He'd only found out when he'd been handed Jesse's possessions, which included the contract, at the hospital after he died.

He stuffed back the chaotic feelings from that day and locked them down tight. "You knew my brother."

"Knew?" Her breath seemed to pause, waiting for his reply.

He braced himself and kept his voice neutral. "Jesse was killed in the same accident where you received your injuries."

"Someone was killed?" Her words were strangled.

Her mother fussed with her hand, patting and stroking. "Darling, let's not worry about this while you're recovering."

April ignored the woman and looked at him, her gaze steady. "Tell me what happened."

Bringing the details to mind, Seth swallowed the emotion, refusing to let strangers see his private grief. "The two of you were at a lawyer's office. You signed a contract about the Lighthouse Hotel. You left together. There was an accident."

"Oh, God," she whispered. "Who was driving?"

"Jesse."

Her mouth opened and closed again, then she swallowed hard. Her shock seemed real. Perhaps this was the first she'd heard of it. Though even people without amnesia often didn't remember an accident that caused them to lose consciousness, so that didn't shed any new light on the bigger dilemma.

He poured her a glass of water from the jug sitting on her side table and thrust it toward her. Wordlessly, she took it and sipped.

Then she looked up at him, her eyes glistening. "You've lost your brother. I'm so sorry."

Seth clenched his jaw against the grief and her sympathy. "Thank you," he rasped and looked away.

After several long seconds of silence, he heard the bedcovers rustle and glanced back to see April sitting a little straighter in the bed. "Where is the Lighthouse Hotel?" she asked.

She'd changed the subject, guiding it away for his sake. He might not trust her, but he instinctively knew she'd done this from kindness. He appreciated it, but it wouldn't make him let his guard down an inch.

He cleared his throat. "In Queensport, on the Connecticut coast."

"Did I have enough money to buy a hotel there?" She looked from him to her mother and back again. "It must have cost a fortune."

"You didn't pay cash," he said, watching her for any indications of prior knowledge. For a mistake in her act. "The contract was for an exchange."

Mrs. Fairchild swung around, hawklike eyes locked on him. "What did she exchange?"

"A recording studio and a recording label, including the rights to the works of several artists signed by that label." *Worthless.* "I'm sure when you're thinking clearly, you'll want those assets back, so if you sign this contract, we can fix it all now." He retrieved the papers from her fingers and unfolded them before placing them and a pen on the wheeled table that was high enough to swing over her bed.

"Yes, darling," her mother said, with an overencouraging smile. "Sign the papers. You love that label. You've spent six years building it up. And your studio—you had it built to your own specifications. It's exactly the way you wanted your work space to be, not to mention it's underneath your house. Your own *home.* I'm not sure what this man's brother said or did to make you sign away your home, your *career,* but let's clear it all up now." She picked up the pen and handed it purposefully to her daughter.

April refused to take the pen, and instead of speaking to her mother, she looked at him—captured his gaze as she cocked her head to the side. "But I must have had a reason for making that agreement."

Her mother patted her hand. "You were exhausted. We were worried you were burned out. Perhaps you just wanted a change and acted rashly. And," she said with raised eyebrows, "we have no idea what that man did to convince you."

Seth would lay serious money on it being the other way around. The Lighthouse Hotel was hundreds of times more valuable than the label and studio. On hearing of the deal, he'd assumed she'd slept with Jesse, used pillow talk to convince him. Jesse had always been a sucker for a gorgeous woman, had spent his entire adult life playing the fool for them—buying women cars or jewelry. This situation was likely no different.

But now he'd never know for sure.

April refolded the papers and pushed them to the edge of the table, then crossed her arms under her breasts. "I can't sign these. I'm sorry, Mr. Kentrell, but I know nothing about you or your hotel. And I'm not reversing anything until I remember why I signed that contract in the first place."

Seth clamped down on the frustration that started to creep through his blood. He needed that hotel and he didn't have time for games. The transaction needed to be reversed before the board members found out.

Straightening, he shifted his shoulders back. "I'll give you twenty-four hours to sign, and then we play hard-ball."

"Hardball?" April asked, eyes wary.

"Your mother thinks you were burned out before you went to the lawyer's office. How many other witnesses do you think I could find to tell a judge you weren't in the right frame of mind? Unstable—mentally unfit to sign a contract. One of my lawyers thinks Jesse didn't have the authority to sign a contract involving that amount of money. I'm willing to bet he's right. Either way, I'll get the contract voided, but I'm sure you don't want your fans to get wind of the word *unstable*."

Her mother, who'd been silently complicit while he was talking, suddenly whipped around. "No." Then back to her daughter. "Sign the papers, April. *Please*."

She sucked her bottom lip into her mouth, looking back and forth between them, and he thought it was over, she was about to sign. Then, as if a regal air had descended to cloak her body, her entire demeanor changed. She was trying to gain the upper hand.

Chestnut-brown eyes locked on his. "I can't. But I promise, Mr. Kentrell, I'll work hard on getting my memory back. I'll do everything the doctors suggest, plus more besides. And when I do, you'll be among the first to know."

She thought he'd sit back and wait, what, days or weeks? *Months?* Either this woman really did have amnesia, or she'd never heard of him before. Sitting back and waiting was so far from his modus operandi that they weren't even in the same universe.

His legal team would continue with their brief to get the contract voided, and in the meantime, he wasn't letting April Fairchild out of his sight. If she really had amnesia, he'd make sure she worked persistently at recovering her memory. And if she didn't have amnesia, then he'd be there when she tripped up.

He sank his hands into his pockets, his course chosen.

"I'll tell you what. I'll help you get your memory back. I won't be *among* the first to know you've remembered. I'll *be* the first."

Surprise widened her eyes, but she recovered quickly. The tip of her tongue rested on the edge of her front teeth as she nodded, considering. "If you want to help, there's something you can do. I want to see the Lighthouse Hotel. I want to see the building that led to this whole…mess."

Her mother started to protest that April needed to be at home, around the people who loved her, but Seth and April both ignored her. April's request suited his plan down to the ground, having her on his territory, in a place where he'd be able to control the situation. The facilities in the presidential suite were more than sufficient to form a work base. He'd be able to keep a proper eye on her, with minimal disruption to himself.

His smile was lazy, assured. "It would be my pleasure."

TWO

Five days later, April sat on the edge of her hospital bed, dressed in casual pants and a pale blue sweater, waiting. The doctors had said she was physically well enough to leave, as long as she took it easy. Even though she hadn't had any more flashes of memory since the day Seth Kentrell had been in her room, they said there was no reason it wouldn't return in time.

They'd also recommended she go to her own home, surround herself with the familiar. The idea held no appeal—she felt no link to descriptions of her house or the woman who maintained she was her mother. Yet something compelling and irresistible was drawing her to the Lighthouse Hotel. She had no idea if she'd even seen it before, but there was a magnetic pull she couldn't deny.

Or even understand.

Perhaps because it had been a meeting about this hotel that had cost a man's life. And her memory.

Something was also telling her she could trust Seth. He'd been open in his agenda, honest in a way that she suspected her mother hadn't been.

As he'd promised, Seth arrived to pick her up. He strode into the room, tall and confident, as if collecting strangers from the hospital was nothing out of the ordinary in his life.

The thought made her frown. How could she possibly know what was normal in anyone's life, let alone Seth Kentrell's? She'd spent five days trying to remember something, *anything* about herself or her life. The medical staff had told her not to push; it would come when she was ready. So she'd tried to follow their instructions to be patient. And when she'd let her mind drift, instead of finding the secrets of her past, it invariably drifted to Seth Kentrell. To the way her body had almost quivered with awareness when he'd carried her in his strong arms. The way his scent had surrounded her when she'd been pressed against him. The way her skin had tingled when he'd reached over her to ring for the nurse.

She gazed at him now as he calmly took instructions from the nurse about not stressing her. Had she felt this way before about a man she'd just met? Perhaps she was the type of woman who formed impulsive attractions. Who fell in love at first sight and was regularly whisked away by sophisticated men.

But she didn't *feel* like that sort of woman. She felt more…guarded than that. Perhaps it was just Seth Kentrell himself who caused the effect in women?

The nurse finished and left the room, and Seth turned. The instant his gaze met hers, she was again hit with the intensity of his navy blue eyes. He held the look, and for one magic moment she had the distinct impression he felt the same tug. But there was a challenge in his eyes, too. He still didn't believe her—that she'd lost her memory, that she couldn't remember signing the contract for his hotel. But at least he was honest about it—and again, paradoxically, his lack of trust made her feel safe with him.

She broke away and looked down. "This is all I have," she said, indicating the small, brand-name suitcase filled with the things she'd had in her drawers.

He rocked back on his heels, his eyes watchful, still assessing. "Despite your mother's pleas that I renege and not take you to Queensport, she's packed a bag for you. It's already been sent ahead."

Her skin pricked. Would he gauge everything she said and did to see if she was faking? But worse was that his words highlighted her feeling of dependence. Needing him to take her to the hotel she wanted to see, needing her mother to pack some clothes. The sooner her memory returned and she took charge of her own life, the better.

She picked up her small suitcase. "I'm ready to go."

"The hospital's allowing us to leave by a little used staff entrance, so we can bypass the media pack out the front." He took the bag from her fingers as a stocky man in a hospital uniform appeared with a wheelchair.

Determined to at least have enough independence to leave the hospital under her own steam, she shook her head. "I'm more than capable of walking to a car."

"Sorry, ma'am," the hospital worker said. "Hospital policy."

Seth stepped forward and laid a hand on the wheelchair's handle. "I'll take her." The other man nodded at Seth and left the room.

Seth politely indicated her seat with a wave of his hand, as if the contraption was a reasonable mode of transport. "Shall we?"

April bit down on her lip. Having medical staff push her in a wheelchair was one thing; but having this man—a man who overwhelmed her, yet only wanted an asset back—do the same, was frustrating. Closing her eyes, she took a breath and let it go. No matter how she wished she had her memories and could resume her life, this was the position she was in for the moment, and fighting it wouldn't help. She opened her eyes and sat in the chair.

When they reached the hidden entrance, he told her to wait while he went for his car, then appeared again minutes later in a sleek, midnight-blue sedan. He held the door open, waiting while she buckled herself in, before closing it and rounding the car.

Seth slid into the driver's seat and, as he smoothly joined the stream of cars, a dark suburban pulled out behind them. The move had been far from covert so it wasn't alarming, but she watched its progress in her side mirror. Did Seth have bodyguards? Did she?

"Who's that following us?" she asked.

"Your security detail. They've agreed to work with hotel security while you're in Queensport. You won't even notice them." He reached behind into the back. "This is for you," he said, passing her a folder.

Drawing her eyes from the side mirror, she opened the folder and scanned the first page: *Background Report: April Fairchild.*

"What's this?"

"I had my staff put it together. To jog your memory," he said, his face inscrutable.

His attention remained on the road and traffic, which gave her an unobserved moment to stare at the folder on her lap. She'd been wanting to know more, desperate even, but now that she had information literally at her fingertips, her shoulders tensed and she had to force herself to open it, to ignore the fear of what she'd find.

She turned past the title page and her lips parted in surprise. Page Two had a biography with a photo that was undeniably of her, but nothing like the reflection she'd been seeing in the hospital mirror. This version of her had professionally styled hair, long and sleek. The colors were the same mix of autumn browns and golds, but it sat perfectly. She ran a finger over the picture on the page. There had obviously been a makeup artist as well—though it was subtle, she looked more beautiful. Her good features highlighted, her faults minimized.

Jazz singer April Fairchild burst onto the scene as a thirteen-year-old, and her fan base has only grown stronger and larger over the past fifteen years. The daughter of a small-time jazz singer, the late George Fairchild...

Her father was dead? Yes, she could feel the deep, stark hollowness in her chest that his passing had left. They'd been close—even without remembering him, she knew that. And for some reason she hadn't asked her mother about him since she'd awoken, as if part of her had known.

...she began her career performing duets with her father, April playing the piano and George on the guitar. Her ability to attract crossover fans has been the key to her phenomenal success...

April flicked to the next page, looking for something, anything, she felt a connection with—that felt real. Photos of her at an awards night, dressed in a sparkling gown, on the arm of a man in a tuxedo she didn't recognize.

More pages, more facts about her career, more photos of her. For twenty minutes she read, absorbed in what felt like the life of another woman. But it had all happened to her. Besides her reaction to her father's death, nothing else had sparked any kind of memory or emotional acknowledgment.

When she'd finished the last page, feeling a little wrung out, she closed the folder and let it lie on her lap.

Seth's eyes flicked over at the movement, and then returned to the road. "Finished?" he asked, voice deep and smooth.

"Thank you, I appreciate this information." She knew he was doing it for his own ends, but that didn't detract from its value to her.

"Any of it familiar?"

She hesitated, debating how much to share about something so personal. But if he was to help her regain her memory, she needed to be honest. She stroked her fingertips across the folder's cover. "My father. I felt something when I read that he'd died."

He didn't react even by a flicker of an eyelash. "You remember him?"

"Nothing that strong. No." How to explain the powerful yet hazy sensation she'd felt? "I just knew it was true that he's dead."

"That was the only familiar part?" There was a cynical twist to his mouth.

"You still don't believe I can't remember?"

Seth shrugged his broad shoulders, his eyes on the road ahead. "I've made my way in the world by never accepting things at face value."

She took in the too-casual way he'd shrugged, the tense set of his jaw, and something underscoring his words that was just out of her reach. There was more to that statement.

She held the seat belt in one hand and twisted to face him. "People have judged you in the past by something false?"

"You could say that." Again, the tension in his body belied his offhanded tone.

"If I were to get my staff to make a dossier like this—" she lifted the report he'd given her "—on you, what would I find?"

"The usual mix of media lies and half stories," he said, seemingly unconcerned by the prospect.

"But if they dug?"

His mouth curved into a sardonic half smile. "I'm sure they'll find the story of my parents. It's something of an open secret."

Despite the heavy subject matter, a sliver of something close to contentment stole through her body. This was the first real conversation she'd had since waking. Besides Seth's first visit to the hospital, each time she'd spoken to someone, it'd been about her physical condition. A discussion felt surprisingly good.

She settled back into her seat and watched him drive. "Since my history is already on the table, why don't you save me the effort of having a dossier made and tell me?"

"With or without the lies and half stories?" he asked with one eyebrow raised.

She bit down on her lip. There was an old, harsh pain he was masking, and it called to a place deep inside her. "Whichever you prefer," she said softly.

A long minute of silence sat between them and she thought he wouldn't answer. But she waited anyway. Then he spoke.

"My brother, Jesse—" he paused and swallowed "—and I are the sons of Warner Bramson. Assuming you don't know who he was, Warner Bramson was a billionaire and a business genius."

She cocked her head to the side. It was a strange way to refer to his father, saying they were the "sons of Warner Bramson."

"Didn't you know him?"

"I knew him very well," he said, voice even. "He spent a lot of time with us."

April tapped a finger against the seat belt she held as she watched him. Perhaps she'd be this interested in anyone's past, now that she'd forgotten her own, but she suspected it was some indefinable quality about Seth Kentrell that was drawing her in.

She pieced together the information he'd given her so far—and came up with a picture that didn't gel. "What am I missing?"

Seth spared her a quick glance, but his expression gave nothing away. "He spent more time with us than he did with his wife and legitimate son."

"Oh," she said on a long breath, as it all made sense.

He nodded once.

"Did you know your half brother well?"

"I met him properly for the first time while you were in the hospital. There was a story on it in the papers. Make sure you get your assistant to dig it out for the dossier she'll make about me." His tone was an attempt at wry humor, but she wasn't buying into it. Despite his efforts to play it down, she knew this was important. Her accident had been almost two weeks ago. The accident that had killed Seth's brother.

She wet her dry lips. "You met at Jesse's funeral."

"Yes," he said as he smoothly took a corner. "And we talked afterward. Have you been to New England before?"

She tried to remember, but nothing came to mind, and the scenery out the window didn't look familiar. "I don't know," she said, glancing across at Seth. He was eyeing her sharply.

The question had been a test.

Her chest deflated. But he had a right to be checking—he had a hotel at stake and absolutely no reason to trust her. She was as much a stranger to him as he was to her, and she'd been involved in his brother's death. She looked back at the green scenery flashing past the window, but then a thought struck.

Was she a stranger to him?

She dragged in a breath. What if the strength of her physical reaction was because she *had* known him? Her body could have been in his arms before and he wasn't telling her. Perhaps they'd been involved and he no longer wanted her, so was keeping his distance now. Or their discussions about her ownership of the hotel would be complicated by her knowing they'd been lovers.

They *could* have been lovers.

She had to ask, had to know. There was no point trying to trick or test him—he wasn't a man to let go of control enough to be caught napping.

She ironed down the fabric of the trousers covering her thighs. "You said we'd never met before the day you came to my bedside."

"That's right," he said, nodding once.

She watched him for a long moment as he skillfully guided the car around a corner. Then she drew a deep breath and plunged in. "It doesn't feel like we've just met."

For a split second his eyes widened, but he covered it so quickly she would have missed it, had she not been watching for a reaction.

When he replied, his voice was smooth and calm as always. "How does it feel?"

"I don't know." She nibbled on her lip. "Like something already exists between us."

He slid her a heavy-lidded look before returning his eyes to the road. "Define 'something.'"

"When you look at me, I…" She trailed off, not really sure how to explain, wishing he'd help instead of grilling her. She moved in her seat, as if that could alleviate the uncomfortable feeling in her stomach. There was something between them, new or existing. He must know it.

"You what?" Seth asked, voice huskier than it had been minutes before.

Her throat felt suddenly dry, but she forced it to work. "It's like we have a…a connection. Already."

Seth's chest expanded rapidly with a breath, but his voice had returned to normal. "As much as I'd like to have had a 'connection' with you, I'm afraid this is just garden variety attraction."

This was a mere attraction? "Do you often have attractions like this?"

He hesitated then cleared his throat before replying. "No."

"And yet," she said, collecting her jumbled thoughts, settling her racing pulse, "you called this a garden variety one."

His hands on the wheel clenched and released before he nodded curtly. "I stand corrected. We seem to have quite a strong attraction." He signaled before overtaking an RV. "But that's all it is. I give you my word we never met before that day in the hospital."

"I believe you," she said, barely above a whisper. And she did. She may not know much about him, but he had a core of honor. If he said they hadn't met, they hadn't.

But she couldn't become involved with someone when her mind was such a scramble. She clasped her hands on her lap. "Since we're talking about this, I have to tell you that it's…problematic for me."

"You find your attraction to me *problematic?*" His lips quirked up at their ends.

She opened her mouth to reply when she realized he was teasing her. She blinked. Seth Kentrell was capable of teasing? Based on their earlier interactions, she wouldn't have guessed it possible. For some reason, it made a bubble of joy form in her chest.

"I'm sorry, did you have plans for us to form a relationship?" she asked, deadpan, teasing him back.

His smile was brief before he frowned. "The idea of a relationship between us would be as *problematic* for me as for you. More so. I just need my hotel back, April."

She flinched inwardly. It was what she wanted to hear; but still, the brush-off hurt a little. She should be grateful they were on the same page. Should be. And she would be.

She straightened her spine as much as she could in the car seat. "So, no acting on this. Agreed?"

He met her eyes for the briefest of moments before returning them to the road ahead. "Agreed."

But as she sneaked a look at him, she wondered if he was able to shut off a response as easily as he implied. She wasn't so sure she had that level of self-discipline—to repress an attraction she felt so keenly.

But she *would*. From this moment.

They talked for the rest of the trip to Queensport about less loaded topics than Seth's family, her lack of memory or their attraction.

When Seth pulled up in the paved area at the front of the Lighthouse Hotel's entrance, April looked around in wonder. It was beautiful—historic and grand. Three stories high in most places, with large windows and gables adorning the front. At one end was the tall lighthouse, built of the same large pieces of roughly hewn stone as the main building. It looked over the paved area where they stood, across a grassy, ten-foot-high cliff out to the sea.

A porter came to take their bags, then a valet took Seth's car. April gazed out at the water's wind-whipped surface and breathed in the salty air. A small part of the tension in her shoulders lifted—tension she'd been carrying since she'd woken to see Seth and her mother in her hospital room. And she started to believe there really might be answers here for her.

She turned back at the sound of voices and saw Seth holding his hand out to a tall, lean man with closely cropped silver hair and intelligent eyes. "April, this is Oscar Wainwright, the manager of the Lighthouse Hotel. Oscar, I'm sure someone as famous as April Fairchild needs no introduction."

Oscar beamed. "Certainly not. We're honored to have you, Ms. Fairchild."

"Oscar…" Seth's voice dropped, became more serious. "I need to apprise you of two sensitive issues. Perhaps we could go into your office."

Keen to accommodate, Oscar led the way. Seth again offered her his arm but she was feeling fine so she shook her head. Besides, since the day he'd carried her in his arms, she'd played over the feeling of being close to him, touching him, in her mind too many times. She didn't want to create more memories to infiltrate her subconscious.

Seth followed her—a pace behind, again as if prepared to be there if she needed him—as they walked to an office not far from the entrance. Although his shadowing of her jutted up against her desire for independence, there was something…*nice* about having Seth walking close. She was too aware of him for it to be comfortable, but she liked the feel of him beside her.

Oscar showed them to high-backed seats before taking his place behind a massive oak desk.

Seth held her elbow as she sat down then took his own seat and faced his employee. "We'll be here three nights."

Oscar nodded. "I've had the two connecting presidential suites prepared."

Her heart skipped a beat. He'd booked connecting suites? Had she misread the situation and his intentions, his meaning during the conversation in the car about attraction? His words from the hospital replayed—I won't be *among* the first to know you've remembered. I'll *be* the first." She relaxed a fraction. He wanted his hotel back, and for that he needed her memory so he could negotiate with her. Of course he'd want to be nearby during their stay. It was reasonable.

"Given the media coverage," Seth said, "you would have heard about Ms. Fairchild's recent accident."

Oscar looked at April with somber features. "My wife and I were very sorry to see the news reports. She's a huge fan of your work, as am I."

"Thank you," April said.

Oscar turned back to Seth, genuine sympathy creating creases around his eyes. "And I was devastated to hear of your brother's passing. He may not have been a regular here, but he was held in high esteem."

"I appreciate that." Seth gave a quick, tense smile then cleared his throat. "The first matter is that Ms. Fairchild's memory was affected by the accident."

"Affected?" Oscar asked.

April nodded. "I'm afraid I can't remember anything much."

"Oh, I'm sorry to hear that."

Seth crossed one ankle to rest on the opposite knee,

bringing the focus back to him. "We'd rather it didn't become public knowledge at this stage, so I'd appreciate it if you put some special rules in place with your staff."

"Certainly." He pulled a yellow legal pad to the center of his desk and picked up a pen.

"Tell them Ms. Fairchild is having some recuperation time after her accident and needs to be left alone. No polite questions, no conversations, no autographs. They speak only when spoken to, and only on matters regarding her stay."

A warm glow filled her chest. She knew she should feel piqued that Seth was arranging things for her, but she couldn't. Instead, she was relieved he'd protected her from polite inquiries that she wouldn't necessarily be able to field. And grateful he'd thought to do it for her.

The manager made a note on the legal pad. "I'll do so immediately."

"Second, it seems that Jesse and Ms. Fairchild signed a contract on the day of their accident regarding the Lighthouse Hotel. The validity of the contract is still in question, but in the meantime, Ms. Fairchild is to be treated with the respect she'd be given if she owned the property and any requests—such as to see behind-the-scenes operations—are to be granted. All decisions will still go through your line manager at Bramson Holdings until this matter is resolved, but technically, she's the owner-in-waiting. And I don't have to tell you that discretion is of the utmost importance, even from your line manager."

"Of course, Mr. Kentrell." Oscar didn't make a note of this one.

"Thank you, Oscar. I apologize for the brevity of this meeting, but I need to take Ms. Fairchild to her suite. We've come straight from her hospital room."

"Ms. Fairchild's health is our main concern," the manager said, offering her a concerned smile. "I'll call a concierge."

Oscar left the room and April turned to Seth. "Thank you."

"For what?" He raised an eyebrow.

"You didn't need to tell him about the contract. I thought you'd keep that under wraps until a final decision was made. If you get the hotel back, no one ever need know."

He frowned. "Even though the contract doesn't take effect until the end of the month, and it may not stand up, you're possibly the current legal owner. It was the right thing to do to inform the manager. You deserve to be treated as such."

"I appreciate it," she said, eyeing him curiously. She was getting the feeling Seth Kentrell always did the right thing. A couple of times since she'd met him there had been deeper, darker emotions flaring in his navy blue eyes, but he'd quickly leashed them before they had time to manifest. He held himself in such control.

A concierge in a dark green uniform arrived to show them to their suites, and once again Seth followed her closely, there if he was needed. Regardless of what else was between them with the hotel issue, one thing she knew for sure, physically she was in safe hands. He wouldn't let her fall.

Warmed by the idea, she walked through the lobby to a pretty glass elevator, but then, as they continued along the hall three floors up, an amorphous thought intruded. There was a definite feeling of…something. Like déjà vu, it was on the edges of her consciousness, just out of grasp. She looked at the walls, the doors they passed, taking in every detail, every potential clue. But the feeling faded and she was left with nothing more than misty remnants of a half-formed idea. And disappointment that a memory had again slipped beyond her reach just as she'd begun to touch it.

Seth tipped the concierge and stood at April's door, hands deep in his pockets. "Have a rest. Your legs must be tired. They're unused to this much movement."

As he said the words, fatigue suffused her limbs. She'd spent most of the morning sitting in a car and in Oscar's office, but she wasn't yet back to full strength. "Perhaps a nap would be good," she conceded.

"When you're ready, knock on my door." He pointed to a door on the inside west wall. "I'll be working in my suite through there. Or ring the operator and ask to be put through to me." His gaze dropped from her eyes to her lips. "I'll be waiting."

Three

April slept soundly through the afternoon and night and woke early, feeling refreshed and eager to explore her new surroundings. After a quick shower, she found a note slipped under the door connecting her suite to Seth's.

Let me know when you're ready for breakfast. S

She gripped the note, undecided. This hotel had pulled at her, had been inextricably linked to losing her memory, and she'd needed Seth to bring her here. She knew he wanted to keep her close—mainly to ensure she wasn't trying to hoodwink him—but did that mean he intended them to spend all their time together?

Part of her wanted the freedom to explore at her own pace, to investigate the crumbs of memories she knew were here. Besides one visit to her hospital bed, and the drive out, he was a stranger—albeit a stranger with whom she shared an inconvenient attraction. Perhaps it'd be best if she took it from here, not rely on him.

Then again, at the moment, even her own mother felt like a stranger. And despite knowing it was unwise, she trusted Seth Kentrell. A vision of his dark beauty rose in her mind. The lure of him, of being near the electric field that seemed to surround him, was just as strong as the lure of exploring on her own. Perhaps stronger.

That banked fire in his eyes both made her wary and called to her on a primal level. If he ever tried to kiss her, would she have it within her to resist? Her skin quivered. Would she want to?

She lifted her hand and hesitated only a second before knocking on his door.

Confident footsteps sounded on the other side before it swung open. Seth stood there, radiating heat and masculinity, and she forgot to breathe. She'd been right to be wary of him. This was not a man to play with, or to underestimate.

"Good morning, April," he said, voice as smooth as matured whiskey. "Did you sleep well?"

She took a deep breath, drinking in his forest-fresh scent, glad she'd decided to see him despite the danger. "I slept right through. My body is obviously still healing."

"We'll take it easy." He ushered her through to his room's dining suite. "I thought you might prefer breakfast here, instead of under the prying eyes in the restaurant."

There was that pattern of doing the right thing by her again. "That was considerate."

"I've been known to be considerate before. On occasion." One end of his mouth hitched, almost a grin, but not quite.

He passed her the menu but she shook her head. "Just toast, please. My appetite hasn't returned properly yet."

Seth picked up the phone and placed their orders before inviting her to sit on the overstuffed couch. "I wonder if you'd like a tour of the hotel today?"

She sank into the couch, then looked up at him. "Surely you don't have the time to play guide to me. You have a large business to run."

"This *is* my business." He lowered himself onto the couch beside her, resting his arm along the back. "I need your memory to return so we can freely discuss the ownership of this hotel, and I can go back to the task of running it and the others."

She smiled wryly. "I'm the fly in your ointment that needs extraction."

The half grin returned for an instant before being pulled back into a smooth smile. "I prefer to think of you as my focus for the time being. A pleasant focus, if you don't mind me saying."

April studied his face. He was using charm to disarm her, trading on their acknowledged attraction, and regardless of how it set her stomach aflutter, she couldn't forget its purpose. He'd just admitted he needed her to give the hotel back, so he was trying to eliminate any adversarial elements to their relationship, making her believe they were after the same thing, on the same team.

To get what he wanted.

She smiled the same smooth smile he'd granted her. "So what do you have in mind for your day with your *focus* then?"

His raised eyebrow said he knew she was aware of his strategy, and it didn't faze him. "I thought, after breakfast I could give you a tour of the hotel. Perhaps it'll remind you of why you wanted to buy it. Or you'll see it's just a hotel, hardly worth your bother."

She batted her lashes. "Thoughtful of you to consider my needs so selflessly."

"I thought so." His dark blue eyes twinkled with amusement. "Some more documents you might find interesting have arrived." He reached to the side table and picked up several thick reports, then handed her the first one. "This is a guide to the day-to-day running of the Lighthouse Hotel."

April took it and leafed through. It seemed to be designed to scare her with charts, tables and spreadsheets. Sewerage problems, bottles of mustard ordered, roof repairs, employee pension plans.

He passed her a second report. "A summary of the assets you relinquished in exchange."

She took the second report and opened to the first page. A photo of her at the piano, singing. And photos of a modern steel-and-glass house, and a state-of-the-art studio—obviously her home. It didn't look familiar. The next pages had a list of the artists signed to her label, Fairchild Creative, along with the songs they'd released and pictures of their CD covers—though she noted her own songs weren't listed. She must have kept the rights to those.

Whoever had put these reports together had done a good job of making one look more attractive than the other—following what were surely Seth's orders.

A knock at the door and the call of "room service" brought Seth to his feet. While he was unaware of her scrutiny, April watched him guide the young man in. He moved with masculine elegance, but also with stark efficiency—not wasting a single movement as he signed the bill and showed the man out.

He may be charming, but he was playing hardball. Playing for keeps.

She couldn't forget that.

* * *

Seth watched April finish her toast. She looked better today—more color in her peaches-and-cream complexion. He'd dreamed last night of touching that skin, finding out whether it was as soft as it looked.

She wiped her hands on a napkin. "If you've finished, I'd like to have a look around."

Interesting, that she didn't have the same enthusiasm for her own house. Once again he wondered about the reality of her amnesia. Surely someone without a memory wouldn't want an unfamiliar setting to be their first port of call?

"Such enthusiasm for a hotel," he said mildly.

"I know what you're thinking," she said, and the look in her eye said she had taken in his full meaning. "But reading through that dossier you gave me in the car, nothing seemed familiar besides grief for my father. Nothing else called to me. Even my own mother may as well be a stranger. But the Lighthouse Hotel—" she looked out the window to the windswept coastline "—there's just *something*."

"Perhaps Jesse showed you photos of it when you signed the contract. Then it would have been one of the last things you saw before the accident. That could explain the impact."

"Careful, Mr. Kentrell. Any more suggestions like that and I'd be inclined to think you actually believe I've lost my memory."

"It's called 'the benefit of the doubt,' Ms. Fairchild."

She considered him for a moment in silence. "It is. But it's not a courtesy I expected you to extend to me."

"I'll admit I have my reservations," he said, choosing his words carefully. "Your amnesia is very convenient."

"Convenient in what way?" She frowned. "If I've just bought a hotel, as you say, why wouldn't I want to just take possession?"

He leaned back in his chair. "Perhaps you're being cautious."

"Cautious? I have a signed contract."

"Your legal team may require time to build their defense," he said, and watched her closely for a sign that he'd hit his mark. He was fairly sure this was her plan, but some part of him hoped it wasn't. That she was as honest as she appeared.

"Ah. My defense." Her smile was heavily laced with irony. "In the same way your legal team is at this moment mounting a challenge to the contract."

He shrugged one shoulder. Of course he had his people on that.

"Then, if I have lost my memory, it's more convenient for you than me. You have this time to prepare, but I'm in the dark and will be scrambling once my memory returns."

A flicker of unease moved in his chest. "The easiest thing all around would be for your memory to return—" he emphasized the words to show he still hadn't made up his mind "—so that we could discuss the matter in full, and you could sign the contract I had made up."

"Does one hotel mean so much to you?" She cocked her head to the side. "I lost count of the number of hotels your company had listed in that report."

"One hotel means more than you can understand at the moment."

"Why?"

The last thing he would do was hand her knowledge of his vulnerabilities. He wouldn't tell her that losing this one hotel could mean the difference between keeping the entire company and losing it to his half brother. He picked up a napkin, roughly wiped his hands and threw it onto the table. "Are you ready for a tour?"

She blinked slowly, as if analyzing his change of topic. Then she stood. "Lead the way."

Seth watched April look around the commercial kitchen, focused on her growing frustration. It'd been a similar situation when he'd shown her the concierge desk and the indoor pool. "What is it?"

"I think I've stayed in this hotel before," she said, turning in a slow circle.

He shook his head. "Guests don't have access to the kitchen. And I double-checked with Oscar in case Jesse brought you here to inspect the property before you signed the document—he would have been notified if a celebrity had been here, regardless of whether he was on shift or not. He assures me you haven't entered the building during his eight years as manager."

"There has to be some connection." She rolled her full bottom lip between her teeth and he felt an almost irresistible urge to capture that lip between his own teeth.

He swallowed hard and focused on her question. "It could just be photos and Jesse's descriptions."

"What if I worked here?"

The corners of his mouth lifted in an ironic smile. "You've been a star since you were thirteen. I hardly think you've have time to bus tables for us."

"Could I have performed here?"

"We're not big enough for someone of your caliber. You pretty much burst onto the scene overnight and have been playing big venues since."

"But it doesn't make sense. Why is this place more familiar than anything else about my life? Even if I've been a guest and somehow sneaked into the kitchen, that doesn't explain why it has more impact than photos of my own home."

Her forehead frowned in confusion bordering on distress, and he wanted to draw her into his arms, to soothe her. He rubbed a hand across his chin. Could she be this good an actress?

He let out a long breath. "I don't know. Let's keep going. Maybe something will click."

She nodded absently as Seth led her out of the main building and through the grounds. He paused for a moment to smell the fresh, salty air. The grass beneath their shoes was neatly trimmed, but the grasses along the rugged shoreline were longer and they swayed gently in the sea breeze.

He loved the Lighthouse Hotel. Most of the hotels the company owned were in cities, in the midst of the hustle and bustle of life. Others were on perfect white beaches, filled with tourists sun baking and playing in the surf. But this hotel had its own vibe—secret, mysterious, wild.

The ground was a little uneven, so, knowing she'd barely been able to walk a week ago, he slipped an arm around her waist to steady her. April looked up quizzically, assessing his intent. "You're still not steady on your feet."

She nodded, looking down as she walked, perhaps unused to accepting help from others, despite being surrounded by assistants for fifteen years. "Thank you," she said.

He guided her to the lighthouse and she stopped at its base to look up at the wide, round structure. "It's beautiful," she whispered.

He followed her line of sight, up the roughly cut stones of its structure to the glassed-in room at the top, under a white dome. "I've always thought so," he agreed. "It hasn't been an active lighthouse for years, but it's popular with the guests."

"Can we go up?" Her chestnut-brown eyes were bright with enthusiasm.

"We can, but I don't think your legs would be up to it." It might only be the equivalent of three stories, but that would be too far for her today.

She cast another look up, then met his gaze. "I'm prepared to give it a go."

Seth reluctantly considered the idea. The medical staff had made him promise not to let her overdo it. But how to decide what constituted "overdoing it"? If he were in her shoes he'd want to explore further.

He set his hands on his hips, feet shoulder-width apart. "On one condition. If I think you've pushed yourself far enough, you let me carry you the rest of the way."

She lifted her chin, obviously considering resisting, then she blew out a breath and nodded.

"You don't like relying on people, do you?"

She paused then smiled ruefully. "The strange thing is, I don't remember anything about myself, but I'm about ninety-nine percent sure that's true." She turned to the stone entranceway and spoke over her shoulder. "Thank you for the offer to carry me. It's considerate, but I won't need it."

He held back a smile—her mouth was making promises he didn't think her legs were able to fulfill, but he left it at that.

As they walked slowly up the winding concrete stairs, he had to admire her determination. Regardless of the memory issue, she'd been hospitalized for thirteen days, some of the time she'd been unconscious, and that had to be hell on her body. They'd told him on her discharge that she'd been doing physiotherapy to gain back the muscle condition that being bedridden for almost two weeks had lost, but she wouldn't be near the condition she would have been in before the accident. And still she pushed herself on to climb the stairs.

He also admired the view of her body as she walked two steps ahead of him. The sway of her rounded hips, the shape of her back under the sky-blue blouse, the jut of a buttock as she lifted a leg for the next step.

Just before halfway, April's steps became labored, slower.

He wanted to scoop her up and take her to the top, save her the struggle. But she wouldn't appreciate it. Instead, he offered her the choice. "Will I carry you?"

"No, I'll be fine." But her voice sounded a little breathless.

He followed, now noticing her body less, and instead listening to the sound of her breath. They were almost two thirds of the way up when he couldn't remain inactive any longer.

"I'll carry you."

"No," she said turning. "I'll be able to do it on my own, I promise." She turned back and on the next step, she stumbled and fell back against him. He grasped her tight against his body, steadying her, taking her weight.

She held herself still for long moments, until he said, "You've been unwell, April. Let someone help. Lean on me."

And then she did, letting the hips and back and the rounded buttocks he'd been watching melt into his body. His pulse spiked, and it had nothing to do with the exercise of the lighthouse stairs and everything to do with the luscious body molded to his. His skin heated at each point they contacted, and everywhere else besides. This slow burn that had started the moment he'd seen her in the flesh had been growing too fast, too high. He wanted nothing more than to lift her in his arms and kiss that full bottom lip, to coax her into kissing him back.

Would she kiss him despite finding her attraction to him "problematic"?

He closed his eyes and bit back a groan. This woman could jeopardize his entire inheritance. He had to keep the fragile alliances he'd built on Bramson Holdings' board of directors, and if Ms. April Fairchild had her way and he lost the Lighthouse Hotel, he'd lose their faith. He wasn't sure he had enough votes to become the next chairman, even if he retained the hotel, but he would give it everything he had.

And as far as he knew, she could be playing him. There wasn't much he hated more than being made a fool of the way Jesse had been by women. The way his mother had been by his father, a man who loved her. April could have awoken in that hospital bed and seen an opportunity to delay things and buy time for her legal team.

The reasoning sounded weak. And the feel of her body pressed against his was still so overwhelming—the smell of fresh apple in her hair, the weight of her, as if she lay above him in bed....

He'd make himself crazy if he waited another instant. Gritting his teeth, he swept her into his arms and continued up the stairs.

She opened her mouth to object, but must have seen the set of his face, because she fell silent.

The sooner Ms. Fairchild regained her memory—or admitted to having it—the better. The minute that happened he'd negotiate his hotel back, and then he was either walking away with his sanity intact...or taking her to his bed.

April relaxed into Seth's strong embrace. This was the second time he'd carried her. She knew she shouldn't like it so much—but she had to admit she did. There was something very safe about being held by him. It wasn't just his physical strength; there was a core of inner strength that she could feel as surely as the fabric of his shirt under her cheek.

They reached the glassed-in platform at the top and he gently stood her on her feet. The curving vantage point had two well-padded deck chairs positioned to take in the view, and she sank gratefully into the comfort of one, relaxing her burning muscles.

Seth didn't join her. He held the inside rail and leaned in toward the glass surrounding them, almost touching it. She could only see his profile, but even from that she could see the alertness in his gaze, the hunger.

"The Lighthouse Hotel means more to you than just being an asset in your portfolio, doesn't it?"

He didn't turn, but the stiffness in his back spoke volumes. "My father would bring us here for holidays when we were young." The understatement in his words sang its own tune—the loved illegitimate son.

"Was it his favorite hotel?" she asked gently.

Still looking out to sea, he shrugged one shoulder. "Its attraction was it was far enough away from his real family, and secluded enough to not cause too much scandal."

He said the words matter-of-factly, but there had to be pain there, to be someone's dirty little secret. Granting him a modicum of privacy for his pain by not pursuing the topic, April dragged herself to her tired legs and joined him at a nearby window. "It's beautiful here."

"Yes," he said, but he sounded lost in his own thoughts.

She looked from the rugged coastline, where the waves crashed onto the rocks that reached above them, to the woods that surrounded them on three sides. She could hear music—a piano and a guitar. And there were voices, a man and a girl singing in harmony. The words of the song drifted to her, as if on the wind, and a feeling of peace descended.

"What is it?" Seth's urgent voice came from close beside her, even though she hadn't heard him move.

She grabbed his hand and held it tightly, lost in the wonder of the moment. "I remember singing here."

Four

April knocked on the internal door connecting her suite to Seth's, and when he called out, "Come in," she slipped through.

He'd changed into a midnight-blue T-shirt and freshly pressed denims, and suddenly she was fully awake from her three-hour nap. Despite the lighthouse not being particularly high, and Seth having carried her part of the way, she'd been exhausted when they'd returned and had crashed. However, the view of him filling out that outfit was akin to a caffeine jolt, bringing every nerve in her body zinging to life.

When he saw her, Seth set his steaming espresso cup on a polished wood table. "I've got something here you'll want to see."

She couldn't restrain a smile. "Does that line usually work on women?"

The corners of his mouth twitched as he regarded her. "You're feeling better then."

"Much." Unsure of her next words, but knowing she had to say something, she lifted a gold brocade cushion from the couch and examined the fringing. "Thank you for your help this morning. I know—" she paused and met his deep blue gaze "—I know I wasn't always making it easy for you to help me."

He shrugged easily. "I'd be frustrated, too, in your position. Neither of us likes to rely on others. We have that in common."

"Thank you," she said, leaning a hip against the couch. It was kind of him to let her off the hook so easily. The more she came to know this man, the more interesting he became—ruthless yet honorable; playing hardball yet offering genuine courtesy. And sexier than any man had a right to be. She hugged the cushion to her stomach as she looked at him from under her lashes. In different circumstances, she'd want to know him better. Might even want to pursue their attraction and see where it led.

But—she sighed—the circumstances were what they were. Nothing could come of whatever was between them. Everything in her head was a jigsaw puzzle, and if by some miracle she could find a few of the missing pieces, he would still only want this hotel from her.

She laid the cushion down on the couch and brought the conversation back to his announcement. "What have you got to show me?"

"When you said you remembered singing here, I had the staff scour through our footage. We've been recording performances for years, and have kept old videotapes." He picked up his espresso and moved to stand beside a television unit, a certain self-satisfaction in his features. "They found something from fifteen years ago."

Her heart leapt and caught in her throat, making it

difficult to speak. This could be it. The clue she'd been hoping to find.

"A video of me?" she asked in a voice higher than normal. "Can I see it now?" She wrapped her arms tightly around her middle, waiting for his reply.

"I had a video player moved up here while you were resting. The tape is in, ready to go. But I'll get the restaurant to send up some food first—you missed lunch, and I don't want you keeling over at my feet."

She almost laughed. Potentially the biggest breakthrough for her memory, and he thought she might like food first? "I'd prefer to see the tape."

"Sure," he said, but put a blueberry muffin from a basket on his kitchenette counter onto a saucer and handed it to her before he pushed the tape into the player.

April sank into one side of the two-seater couch that faced the television but stayed on the edge, her soft jade skirt pulled taut over her knees. She felt Seth sit beside her, deeper in, but she kept her eyes on the blank screen, nibbling her muffin. Suddenly colors lit the TV set, at first out of focus, then clearing to show a man on the stage, holding an electric guitar. She recognized him from the dossier, but even if she hadn't seen the photo, part of her would have known that man was her father. George Fairchild. Emotion pricked at the back of her eyes. She stopped nibbling the muffin, slowly lowering it to the saucer.

Without a word, he launched into a jazz number that was familiar, even if she couldn't name it. He was good. He wasn't just hitting the notes—the rhythm flowed from his fingers and voice. Entranced, April strained toward the screen.

Seth's voice was close to her ear. "George, your father, had a contract to sing through the summer as a live-in entertainer."

She nodded in acknowledgment of the information but couldn't drag her eyes from the screen. The audience in the ballroom applauded at the end of the song, and once the room fell silent again, her father spoke. "I have a special treat for you tonight. My little girl, April, has been practicing a song for you. She had her thirteenth birthday a couple weeks ago and I promised once she was a teenager we could sing a duet. Let's welcome her out."

The audience clapped and cheered and then a very young version of herself approached, a jumbled mix of nerves and wide-eyed excitement. She could feel that same reaction now—stomach cramped painfully, but bubbling over with anticipation, too—and wondered whether it was because she could see it before her, or whether it was a memory of that time resurfacing. Or perhaps it was just her reaction to the possibility of what she'd see on the tape.

Her father held out a hand and thirteen-year-old April walked over to take it, grinning madly. He kissed the back of her fingers and then released her hand to start playing his guitar. He launched into what she somehow knew was an old Louis Armstrong favorite, and after the first couple of lines, a higher, yet surprisingly strong voice joined his.

April's mouth moved in synch with her thirteen-year-old self—the song still lived in her subconscious. Her eyes filled with tears as she reclaimed part of her soul.

Seth leaned over to whisper, "I checked the dates. This was only a few months before your debut concert with your father in New York. Well, what the world considers your debut. Yet there you are."

"There I am," she repeated, eyes still on the screen.

At the end of the song her father again grasped her

hand, and without thought as she watched the tape, April lifted her hand off her lap. Strong warm fingers threaded through hers as her hand was enveloped in Seth's. She drew her eyes from the screen to look at the man beside her, and a shiver passed along her skin that had nothing to do with the déjà vu from the video. It was all Seth. The heat and the want he effortlessly evoked in her, the naked desire in his eyes.

Then her father spoke again, capturing her attention, and she was dimly aware of Seth removing the saucer and muffin from her hand and setting it aside.

"Thank you. As you can imagine, I'm very proud of her. And now she has one more surprise in store for you." He gave the screen April an encouraging smile and the camera panned out as she walked to a baby grand that had been just off screen.

She sat, fingers hovering over the keyboard in the shape of a chord, as if gathering herself. Then she sounded the chord and her fingers flew confidently into a lively rhythm. The audience broke into applause, and when they quieted, she and her father sang together. George even paused at one point, ceding the limelight to his daughter, and she broke into an enthusiastic scat. The audience seemed astonished and thrilled.

Seth squeezed her hand, bringing her closer on the couch, and April was dimly aware of a tear trailing a path down her cheek. She knew the words, her fingers twitched as if they knew the notes. Then her spine straightened as a thought struck. *Did they?* Would her fingers remember more than her mind?

She turned in the couch, gripping Seth's hand tight. "Is that ballroom still there?"

"It's been refurbished, but it's essentially the same."

Anticipation built in her chest, pulling tight. "What about

the piano?" Finding the very one she'd played as a teenager was a long shot, given there had been a refurbishment, but how wonderful would it be to see it?

"There is a piano there." He glanced at the older ballroom on the screen, as if comparing the instruments. "I'm not sure if it's the same one."

She leapt from the couch, feeling more enthusiasm than she'd felt for anything since she'd woken. "Can we look? Now?"

Despite the risk that she may not remember this any better than she'd remembered the rest of her life, she wanted to try, needed to see if she could play the music she'd heard.

An indulgent grin tugged at the corners of his mouth. "Sure."

While he closed the door behind them, she started down the corridor at a brisk pace. He caught her within a few steps.

"Eager, I see," he said, amusement clear in his voice.

She bit down on her lip, and glanced at him out of the corner of her eye. "I guess I am. This could be significant."

As they stepped into the elevator, she mentally crossed her fingers, hoping it *would* be significant, and not another dead lead, like the reports Seth had commissioned for her, which had sparked no more than a memory that her father was gone. Maybe this would be the catalyst to bring her memories back.

When they reached the ballroom entrance, Seth pushed the double doors open, and even before she set foot in the room, her eyes were drawn to the piano. She stilled—limbs, heart, lungs—unable to move even if she'd wanted to.

It was the same shiny black baby grand she'd watched herself play on the tape.

Seth waited, then took her hand and led her across the room. "Do you want to play it?" he asked gently.

She moistened her lips as her eyes devoured the beautiful piano like a lover. "You don't mind?"

He chuckled and pulled out the stool for her. "You possibly own the hotel. I think we can swing a bit of time on the piano."

She sat down, heart in her mouth, not sure if she would be able to play something as simple as chopsticks. But as her fingers hovered over the keys, it just felt natural to form them into a chord. And then the melody of the song in the video was in her head, and her hands translated it to the baby grand. It felt liberating, as if she'd set her hands free.

When she finished the piece, more music crowded into her mind and she set that free, too. Long and smooth. Fun and energetic. Sad and haunting. Some, she simply played, for others, she sang the words—whatever felt right. And it *all* felt right, felt satisfying in a place deep inside that she'd forgotten existed.

As she launched into an Ella Fitzgerald number, she looked up and saw Seth watching her, a burning heat in his eyes. He leaned back against the wall, hands deep in his trouser pockets, legs crossed at the ankles. The pose of a relaxed man. Yet he was far from peaceful. He radiated tension. She'd been vaguely aware that some hotel staff members had drifted in and formed a small crowd for her performance, but she only had eyes for Seth. For all that heat. She wanted it closer. All of it.

She segued into "Fever" without thinking much about it, and his navy blue eyes burned hotter.

As her fingers touched the final notes of the song and the sound faded, she paused. She and Seth hadn't broken eye contact for endless minutes and the air crackled with their attraction. The staff burst into claps and cheers for the impromptu concert.

Seth cleared his throat. "Okay, everyone back to work." The command had the staff moving quickly, but Seth didn't move a muscle.

Her heart hammered at her ribs as the staff shuffled out, some smiling their gratitude to her, one giving her a thumbs-up. It seemed to take an eternity, and all the time Seth's gaze was locked on her.

The moment the last person left, Seth strode the distance to her, slamming the ballroom door closed on the way past. April watched his progress, hardly daring to breathe. When he reached her, without a word or any preliminaries, he drew her up from the stool and his mouth came down on hers with a fierceness she welcomed with everything inside her. She wound her arms behind his neck, securing him, demanding everything he had to give.

His lips moved with urgency, his tongue claiming her, wanting her. Had she ever been desired this much? She couldn't imagine it was possible. The body heat emanating from him soaked through her clothes, down into her bones. Her skin tingled at every point that his hands, mouth or body touched.

All she could think about was the feel of his broad back beneath her fingers, the curves of his hard muscles, and wanting more, more. The clean forest scent of him blended with something darkly alluring and filled her head. His fingers stabbed through her hair and massaged her scalp, and in this moment she belonged to him, wholly and completely.

His hands slid down to her waist and he effortlessly lifted her high, onto the baby grand. Leaning down to preserve contact with his lips, she opened her thighs, and at the same moment he stepped forward, bunching her long, soft skirt up and pressing against the core of her. She moaned, helpless to do more than kiss and be kissed.

His mouth moved to the side of her lips, to her cheek, and she took the opportunity to gulp in the air her lungs had been screaming for; but she locked her ankles behind him to make sure the break didn't become permanent.

"I can't stand it," he murmured next to her ear. "I want you so badly I can't stand it."

She ran her hands up over his strong shoulders, up the taut muscles of his neck, and pulled his face back to kiss her again. She needed his kiss, needed *him*. She wanted him more than anything. More than finding her memory. More than having this hotel.

Suddenly her body went cold, as dread washed through her. *More than having the hotel?*

With no memory, the last thing she could afford was a case of starry-eyed naivety. And she had the worst suspicion that there might be more behind Seth's attentions than she'd been willing to admit.

Seth was almost mindless with wanting when he noticed the change—her mouth still touched his, but suddenly he was in the kiss alone. He pulled back.

"What's wrong?" he rasped.

April blinked hard, then looked away, and he forced himself to wait while she found her breath.

"I don't know," she said finally, but she still didn't meet his eyes.

Heart thumping hard with his need for her, Seth stepped back and put an arm's length of distance between them. "Yes, you do. Tell me."

She readjusted the neckline of her blouse that he'd pulled to the side. Then she looked him squarely in the eye and spoke softly. "I don't know whether I can trust your intentions."

After being so consumed by the kiss, her sharp accusation came like a knife to the gut. "You think I'm capable of seducing you into signing the contract?"

She didn't flinch, but she seemed to choose her words with care. "I think you're capable of worse, if your business interests are threatened."

About to respond, Seth hesitated. She was right. He'd been called ruthless and single-minded before and he'd deserved the labels. Yet now, when he had the hotel and therefore his career at stake, the only thoughts in his head had been about kissing this woman.

She made him feel so much, enough to drive all thought from his mind. A chill passed along his spine. She made him feel *too* much. It was dangerous.

He liked his relationships with women to be simple and disentangled. Controlled. He decided long ago that he'd be a fool for no one. His mother had been a very public fool for his father, being his mistress for thirty-two years. And Jesse had been used by women for his entire adult life—they'd wanted him to buy them a car or jewelry or to meet people he knew. Jesse hadn't cared; he'd wanted to be seen as the big man. *Damn fool.*

He had to walk away from April quickly—before history repeated itself and he became a fool for her. Emotions this strong led nowhere else. He'd seen it often enough.

But first his honor compelled him to let her know the truth. She deserved it. "The only thought in my mind was kissing you."

Her chestnut eyes were earnest as they looked deeply into his. "We've acknowledged a certain attraction between us."

Her tongue darted out to moisten her lips. "Seth, promise me you won't use that to encourage me to give in on the hotel issue."

Attraction? He almost laughed at the understatement. "April, this isn't merely an attraction for me." He closed his eyes to make the admission come more easily. "I'm sure you've guessed how badly I want you. So badly that when you're near I can't stop the images of you in my bed. But it won't happen. I won't let it."

"It's problematic for you," she said, repeating their phrasing from the car trip.

"Tell me you weren't sleeping with my brother a few weeks ago." Merely saying the words ripped a hole open in his chest, but it had to be said. Needed to be answered.

"I don't think I was," she said uncertainly. Her eyes shifted to the left. She'd wondered the same thing.

His whole body clenched tight and he had to relax his jaw to speak. "You can't guarantee it, though, can you?"

She slid down from the piano, straightening her long skirt as she answered, "No, I can't."

Although he'd expected the words, they still acted as a bucket of ice water over his head. He folded tense arms across his chest. "Convince me you've really lost your memory. Show me some irrefutable proof."

"I can't," she said, her forehead puckered in a frown.

Something inside him pushed farther, wanting to sever the invisible cords that had bound him to her in such a short space of time. He pushed his shoulders back. "Sign the contract to give me my hotel back."

"Seth, you know I can't until I've regained my memory."

"So you say. If you can't guarantee you weren't recently sleeping with my brother, or prove you've lost your memory or sign my hotel back, then do one final thing for me."

"What is it?" she asked warily.

"Stop making me want you more than my next breath." The words were wrenched from his throat. "I refuse to hand over control of what I think and do to a physical desire. I *won't*."

He would *never* be love's fool.

Unable to stand her proximity any longer—especially with his admission hanging in the air—he stalked to the far side of the ballroom. He slammed a hand up high on a round pillar, his back to April. But he felt her follow, bringing her brand of damned temptation with her.

"This isn't what I want either," she said with a slight tremble in her voice. "I don't even know who I am, or if I can trust you fully. But…"

He turned slowly, taking in the picture of her biting down on her bottom lip, trying to contain what she'd been about to say.

"But?" he asked, knowing he should walk away. Run.

She dragged in a breath, then spoke in a rush. "The only things that have made sense since I woke up are playing music and your kiss. They're the only times I've felt right, that I've felt *me*. When you put me up on that piano and filled me with your heat and passion—"

Seth clenched his fists beside him, physically restraining himself from reaching for her again. "Enough," he said, voice ragged.

"You're right." She stood taller, seemed more sure of herself than ever before. "I won't let it happen again, but I can't bring myself to regret it—those few moments of feeling alive, of knowing who I am." Inclining her head, she was dignity and poise personified. "Thank you."

She was *thanking* him? For almost taking her on a piano in a room anyone could have walked into? Not trusting himself to reply, he turned sharply and stalked out of the room. He needed a cold shower, or perhaps to dive into the ocean and purge his body of this unreasonable need.

He'd bring his body back under control if it killed him.

Five

Three days later, April was eating breakfast on her balcony, taking in the sublime views of the blue-gray water stretching to the horizon, when a curt knock came from the internal door that connected her suite to Seth's. Since their explosive kiss in the ballroom, she hadn't seen him once. She'd kept a low profile, spending most of her time on this balcony or wandering the wilderness tracks at the edges of the grounds.

His only contact had been a brief note under her door, informing her that he'd contacted reception and extended their stay from the original three days to an indefinite time frame. When she read the note, part of her had been relieved she'd have more time to remember, but that didn't explain the way her pulse had picked up. That had been about knowing she wouldn't be leaving Seth just yet....

Knowing he was on the other side of a mere wood-and-plaster wall had become like water torture—a slow, constant drip, drip at her sanity. She'd lain in bed at night, tossing, turning, tangled in her sheets, thinking of him only a few feet away in his bed. Wondering if his need was as unquenchable as hers. If he'd locked the door from his side.

If he'd turn her away if she crept through.

She groaned and rubbed the heels of her hands into her eyes. Was she ready to see him now? Could she trust herself to behave like a business acquaintance, when their kiss had taken her yearning for his touch to new heights?

The knock came again, more insistent, and she took a last fortifying sip of her mango juice before padding in her slippers to the interconnecting door. When she swung it open, she didn't look at him, couldn't afford to just yet. So, insides squirming, she turned and retraced her steps back to the balcony.

"Do you mind if I finish my breakfast while you talk?" she asked over her shoulder.

"Of course not." His voice flowed over her, seeping in to fill those parts of her greedy for him, luring her back to her nighttime thoughts. She sat, flicking her sunglasses down to shade her eyes, and picked up her bowl of yogurt with a hand that only trembled a little.

"I see your appetite returned," he said with a trace of a smile in his voice. "Or were you expecting company?"

She surveyed the glass table before her, littered with an empty cereal bowl, the remnants of a fruit platter, her juice glass, buttered toast and two boiled eggs still in their cups. She set the yogurt back down and acknowledged his point. "I'm ravenous. It must be the healing my body is doing." Though she was sure an argument could be made that she was satisfying a hunger that was *safe*.

A hunger that wouldn't cause her heartache.

She risked looking up at him, her own private forbidden

fruit. If she hadn't been sitting already, she might have lost her balance. The light breeze from the ocean danced in his hair and molded his crisp, white shirt to his torso. Their kiss had been too brief—she hadn't had the opportunity to trace the tantalizing lines, to relish the delectable shapes of his chest and arms. She sucked her bottom lip into her mouth. What a squandered opportunity.

She raised her eyes to meet his and felt an electric jolt from the heavy-lidded awareness there. He knew what she was thinking. His gaze traveled to the side of her throat, skimming past her décolletage. She needed his touch, his mouth, wanted what his gaze offered.

He swallowed hard and looked away. Dug his hands into his pockets. "Speaking of expecting company, you have a visitor. Though, since you're not there to meet her, I suspect it's an unexpected visit."

A visitor? She folded back into herself, recoiling from the idea. A visitor would expect her to be someone she couldn't remember how to be—something she wasn't yet ready to face.

Unless it was the other person who knew about her memory loss. "My mother?"

"Yes." He spoke the word with neutrality, but she could tell he hadn't warmed to her. "The concierge just called. Would you like to go down and meet her together?"

Despite the woman being her mother, and having only met the man beside her two weeks ago, she nodded, accepting his offer. With no memories of who her friends were, her options for allies were next to nil. And the time she'd spent in her mother's company had been...tiring. Seth's support was embarrassingly welcome.

"Thank you," she said as she stood. She'd walked back through the sliding glass doors before she realized something was askew in the situation. "Why did the call go to you and not me?"

Unfazed, Seth picked up her suite's key card and handed it to her. "I've instructed the concierge and reception desk to forward all inquiries and requests regarding you to me. You're hardly in a position to be fielding them at the moment."

She opened her mouth to disagree but closed it again. It had only been minutes since she'd been alarmed by the thought of meeting an unknown visitor.

After changing her slippers for sandals, they stepped out of her suite and she let Seth pull the door closed behind them. "Again, thank you. Have there been many calls about me?"

"Mainly journalists wanting an interview or at least some gossip," he said, as they walked down the richly carpeted corridor. "Your agent has been calling regularly, too."

She faltered for a fraction before falling into step with him again. She hadn't even considered that she *had* an agent. Although she shouldn't be surprised. If she had the career that Seth's report had shown her to have, of course she'd have a team of people who would now be looking for her. Her chest constricted. She'd been living here in a little bubble, protected from reality, but she needed to start paying attention to the outside world.

She glanced up at Seth's profile. "What have you told them?"

"That you're not fully recovered and will contact them as soon as you're able." He shrugged one shoulder, as if it was no big deal.

April's fingertips trailed lightly along a brass rail attached to the wall. What would she be doing this minute, if she hadn't been in Jesse's car that day? Meeting with people?

Rehearsing? Then her mind jumped a step further—what would she have been doing all the days since the accident? Her stomach swooped. "Have I missed appointments? Concerts?"

"It's common knowledge you were having a break from performing when the accident happened," Seth said matter-of-factly. They stepped into the small glass elevator and he hit the ground floor button. "The news was in all the papers about six months ago. Perhaps because, as your mother said at the hospital, you were feeling a little burned out. It was good timing in that regard—you haven't missed anything too important."

She sighed in relief that she at least hadn't been remiss in her commitments before another question occurred to her. "There hasn't been a single journalist here at the hotel. If they're ringing and they've been at the hospital, why aren't they interested in being here?"

"They are." He glanced around through the glass as he spoke, forever keeping an eye on the operations of his business. "We have security on the private road leading up to the hotel. Only those with bookings get through. And we've thrown out the guests who were found to be trying for a photo or acting suspiciously."

Before she could process the information, the elevator doors swooshed open to the lobby.

The tall, elegant woman from the hospital saw them, hurried over and flung her arms around her. "Darling!"

April self-consciously raised her arms to return the embrace. "Hello…" *Mother? Mom?* In the hospital, she'd avoided referring to her mother by a direct name or title, and still wasn't sure what she normally called her.

Before she could decide, the woman took her elbow and drew her away from Seth. "I've come to take you home."

April's jaw slackened at the bluntness of the sudden announcement. "I'm not going home yet."

"It's where you belong," her mother said, not dissuaded in the least.

April felt Seth beside her. "Hello, Mrs. Fairchild."

"Good morning, Mr. Kentrell," she said with ice in her voice. "I'm here to collect my daughter."

He merely arched an eyebrow. "And if your daughter doesn't want to be collected?"

Her mother turned to her. "April, has your memory returned?"

Grasping for a way to not admit the truth, she looked from one to the other, but was unable to blatantly lie. "Not beyond hazy snippets."

"Then you're in no fit state to make decisions." She stood closer to April and glared at Seth. "I allowed you to take her from the hospital against my better judgment, but it's gone on long enough now. As a parent, I can't walk away when my child is vulnerable."

"Your child, Mrs. Fairchild, is an adult." Seth's mouth quirked sardonically.

She'd decided on the walk down to the lobby that it was time to step up to the plate about the life she'd been ignoring, but it was too soon to leave the Lighthouse Hotel. She'd been thinking more along the lines of having correspondence forwarded to her, schedules and the like. Familiarizing herself. Not going back. Not until her memory returned.

"She may be an adult," her mother was saying to Seth, "but she can't remember her childhood, her family or what she did last month."

He rocked back on the heels of his shiny black shoes, all calm unconcern. "And yet she does know her own mind. She's neither confused nor foolish."

"I'm sure I could get a court to—"

April interrupted. "I'm staying," she said firmly.

Seth's face remained impassive, but she thought there was a millisecond's flare of satisfaction in his eyes.

Her mother noticed it, too—it was in the way her chin kicked up, the way she folded her arms. "If you're staying, I'm staying, too."

"There's really no need." Without seeming to have moved, Seth was shoulder to shoulder with her, presenting a united front. "I assure you April is safe here and the staff are treating her with every possible care."

"It's not the staff I'm worried about." Her mother's shrewd eyes narrowed at Seth. April frowned. Had her mother seen more in Seth than just the satisfaction in his eyes? Was their attraction obvious to others?

April laid a staying hand on her mother's arm. "Really, Mother, there's no need…"

Seth nodded, then called over the concierge. "Mrs. Fairchild is checking in. Take her to reception and have her booked into our best available suite." Then he murmured extra instructions more quietly and April was distracted by her mother grabbing her elbow again.

"Don't worry, darling," she said with an overly bright smile. "I'll look after you. Everything will be fine now that I'm here."

April nodded because her mother was expecting her to, but unease sat deep in her chest. She tried to rationalize it away—this was the woman who'd raised her—but the awful reality was that the only person she felt comfortable with, could let her guard down with, was a man she knew she shouldn't trust, the man who merely wanted the hotel from her.

She thought back to the video of her father, to her

reaction to him, and wondered if she'd ever felt the same emotional pull for her mother, or had she always felt differently about her parents?

The concierge in his dark green uniform guided her mother away, and Seth moved closer. "Are you okay?" he asked as he scrutinized her face.

A smidgeon of family loyalty appeared and prevented her saying anything about her mother, so she smoothly changed the subject. "What were the extra instructions you gave to the concierge?"

"I told him to have reception put her at the other end of the hotel from us."

April bit down on her lip to stop the laugh, and saw the answering twinkle in Seth's eyes. She glanced over at the woman in question, standing across the room, making the receptionist's life difficult with what were no doubt a list of demands.

Then she looked back to Seth, still standing so close. "But why go to that much trouble? You didn't need to check her in—I was just about to tell her I was fine and she could go."

"Because she was right," he said quietly, still watching her mother, face inscrutable.

Bemused, April thought back over everything her mother had said. "That I can't make decisions for myself?"

He turned to face her, bringing himself near enough to feel the intoxication of his warm breath on her cheek. "That you're in a vulnerable position and you could use someone to look out for you."

"Am I in danger from you?" she asked in a low voice.

"Maybe you are." His eyes fixed on her mouth for a long moment, and her lips came alive, as if he'd grazed them with a finger. "And maybe I'm in as much danger from you."

He turned on his heel and strode from the room, leaving April watching him go, her lips still tingling from the touch of his gaze.

Seth rapped on the interconnecting door that led directly to April's suite and felt his pulse pick up at the prospect of seeing her. It was early, just past 6:00 a.m., but he hadn't seen her alone in two days. Her mother clung like a vine.

At first he'd accepted that it was for the best. She was safe from his voracious need, and her mother would be the better person to help April regain her memory....

He frowned, realizing that he believed April *did* need to regain her memory. In fact, he couldn't remember when he'd last doubted her—not only had she not slipped up once, but he knew now that she had too much integrity to be playing a farce. She'd been telling the truth the whole time.

He straightened. Regardless of her honesty, the time he'd given her alone with her mother had gone on long enough.

He was here to do a job. It was time he regained his hotel.

Setting his freshly made demitasse of espresso on a table nearby, he rapped on the internal door again, louder this time. Being close to her, knowing he couldn't have her—wouldn't let himself—was intolerable. But it would stop today. He had a plan that would suit them both. They could make a new agreement, move on, move out, and both put the entire episode behind them.

All he needed was to see her alone to outline his plan.

He lifted his hand to knock a third time, but the door was pulled open and he was presented with April, luscious, hair mussed, a robe tightly sashed at her waist, her cheek still creased with pillow marks. He dragged in a lungful of air as his body roared to life. She'd just left her bed. It would still be warm with her body heat. His heart thumped hard against his ribs. How would she react if he kissed her? Walked her backward to that still-warm bed, laid her down, pushed her into the mattress with his own body weight?

Unable to stop himself, he reached out, gently running his thumb down her rosy cheek, cupping the side of her face with his palm. Her skin was smooth, silken. Sensuous.

"Seth," she said, her voice husky.

The sound of her voice startled him, as if rousing him from a dream. He dropped his hand and took a deliberate step back—away from the almost unbearable temptation of her.

He cleared his throat, trying to also clear his mind. "I'm sorry for the early hour."

April's knuckles, still gripping the brass doorknob, whitened. Eyes wary, as if she wanted to slide behind the protection of the door, she held herself firm. She had courage, this woman. When she spoke, her voice was steady. "I'm guessing you wanted to see me without being overheard by my minder."

"Actually, yes."

"I can understand. She's quite determined." Her hand on the doorknob relaxed, as if she was more confident knowing they were discussing her mother. "She never lets her guard down, rarely lets me out of her sight."

Seth came to attention. "Is she a problem?"

"She means well," April said after a small hesitation.

He wasn't as sure of that, but he let it go for now. "Have you had any progress with your memory?"

She sighed and pulled her robe's sash tighter, probably not realizing that it pulled more firmly across her breasts. "At first I thought it might help to have her here. That I might remember something about her, or that her memories of our time staying here might prompt something."

He'd hoped the same. He reached for the steaming espresso shot and sipped it to stop his hands from grasping her and enfolding her in his arms.

"But it hasn't?" he said over the rim of the small cup.

"She talks so much about what we did, and my father, that I'm worried that anything I do start to remember will be something she's accidentally planted in my head, instead of a true memory." She shrugged one shoulder—which also pulled the fabric of her robe tighter, but he tried not to let his eyes linger.

"I'm sorry." Perhaps letting her mother stay hadn't been the right thing to do. He could fix that. "Would you like me to send her away?"

She arched an eyebrow and smiled. "I think I can deal with my own mother. But thank you for your offer, Saint George."

The sight of her smile so radiant made something in his chest constrict, and he couldn't suppress a return smile. "Well, if the dragon becomes too much, just say the word and I'll ride in on my white steed."

"I appreciate it." She chuckled. "So, is that why you woke me so early?"

He set his cup down on the side table and rubbed a hand over his chin. "I have a proposition that I think will suit us both. But I need time to outline it to you without worrying about interruptions."

"Sounds intriguing." Her warm brown eyes sparkled.

Everything within him demanded he release the sash at her waist and make those sparkling eyes burn with the scalding heat he knew was within her. Knowing that resisting the urge was the right thing to do was cold comfort, but he resisted nonetheless.

When he trusted himself to speak again, he said, "Can you get away tonight? I'll take you out on the yacht and we'll have dinner."

She bit down on her lip, but the smile peeped through anyway. "No chance of dragons appearing. You're not taking any chances, are you?"

"I've seen her in action. I think only the presence of a moat around our dinner venue will be enough."

She laughed then, fully and without restraint. Such a beautiful sound; and more, it made his heart kick up to see her so relaxed—for a few moments she wasn't worrying, just being. And when her laugh ebbed to a natural end, her eyes still shone bright with the joy.

"What time?" she asked.

Seth had to drag his mind away from her laugh, her mouth, and remember what they were talking about. The yacht. Tonight. Dinner.

"Seven o'clock."

She reached for the doorknob again, either because the conversation was coming to an end or because she'd read the thoughts in his eyes. Then she nodded. "I'll meet you down at the dock. It'll be easier to slip away if I'm alone."

"I'll look forward to it," he said—wishing he wasn't looking forward to it quite so much—and watched her face disappear as she closed the door.

Six

April followed the path to the dock at five minutes to seven, nerves squirming in her stomach. It was a warm night, so she'd chosen a silky violet dress that felt soft against her skin, and brought a thick shawl in case the breeze picked up out on the water.

Up ahead, Seth stood staring out to sea, hands thrust deep in the pockets of his black trousers, the fabric of his crisp, white shirt draping his back. As she drew near he turned, and even from this distance she saw a fire ignite in his eyes.

The heat of that same fire burst to life down low in her belly, kicking her pulse into overdrive. She stopped on the path. Was it wise to be out on the water alone with him at night, when they were so combustible?

A movement caught her eye. Another man busily moving around on one of the three yachts at the dock, in what looked like steps to prepare to sail. She sighed with relief. They wouldn't be alone. Of course. A man like Seth would have staff for the menial tasks wherever he went. She continued walking down the path, partly disappointed, but mainly relieved.

No, she corrected herself, *completely* relieved.

Seth didn't smile when she reached him, didn't seem pleased to see her. The tightly leashed emotion in his eyes went beyond such superficial feelings. *He was burning alive.* She understood; she was right there with him, standing amidst the scorching flames, heart throbbing painfully, limbs heavy with shackled longing.

"You managed to get away," he finally said, voice tight.

She opened her mouth to speak, but no sound came out, no words formed in her head. She blinked then reined in her recalcitrant body, and tried again. "I told my mother I had a headache and was going to bed. Not terribly imaginative, but it worked."

He scrutinized her face, as if checking for any underlying truth to her excuse. "Under the circumstances," he said slowly, "I'm sure a headache was enough to create an effect."

A wave of guilt for potentially worrying her mother descended onto her shoulders. In her desperation to get away, she'd chosen a quick and easy excuse, which in light of her recent history, could cause unnecessary angst. But she forced herself to brush concern aside—her mother's refusal to give her space even when asked had left no other option. She would make a point of telling her mother in the morning that she felt fine.

Seth extended a hand. "Are you ready?"

The yacht bobbed on the water and she could see the sense in having someone steady her as she stepped aboard. But since she wanted more than anything to feel his touch again, to be close enough to smell the scent of his skin, it would be far wiser to step on unaided.

As she was deciding, his resonant, deep voice came from beside her. "Not long ago you were working with a physiotherapist to have the strength to walk again. For safety's sake, let me help you board."

She bit down on her lip and reluctantly conceded his point. "Thank you," she said as she took his outstretched hand, feeling the slide of his warm, roughened palm across the highly sensitized surface of hers. A shiver passed across her skin. He held tightly, keeping her secure, but the pressure felt like a tug on her soul. Not daring to meet his eyes, she stepped onto the yacht, then released his hand.

It seemed to be about forty feet long, sleek and shiny, with soft lights on the mast. A staircase descended below, but on this level, there was a deck toward the front and a solid canopy housing the controls.

The younger man who'd been checking on ropes earlier appeared. "The food is in a picnic basket downstairs, Mr. Kentrell. Champagne's in the ice bucket, the other drinks are in the fridge. Everything's ready for casting off."

"Thank you, Jai," Seth said, approval clear in his voice. The younger man acknowledged the thanks with a smile and left.

As she watched Jai climb back to the dock and get ready to release the rope, her stomach dropped away. She circled her throat with a hand, as if she could fortify herself against reality. "We'll be alone."

His eyes flicked to her. "Utterly."

"Oh," she said on a long breath.

He didn't appear concerned by the prospect, by the danger they courted. He merely raised an eyebrow. "Is that a problem for you?"

"It's not for you?"

His chest seemed to rise and fall a little too frequently, but his voice didn't alter. "I didn't want us to be overheard while we discussed my offer." He glanced to where Jai was waiting to cast off and lowered his voice. "Our arrangements are of a sensitive nature."

She took a small step back. He was right—the only person who knew the situation was her mother. Even the hotel manager had only been given limited information. Since they'd just gone to elaborate lengths to avoid her mother, bringing a young employee along to witness their negotiations would be counterproductive. On a boat this size there would be no guarantee they wouldn't be overheard.

However, there may be another danger—beyond their obvious flammability—in letting young Jai leave. She folded her arms under her breasts. "Can you sail?"

Seth's features were transformed into mock affront. "Can fish swim?"

"Okay then," she said, relaxing a fraction and deciding to take this as it came, "show me what you've got."

Seth stilled—an arm that had been reaching toward the console hung in midair, his torso and limbs frozen. After several beats, he smoothly began to move again, as if he'd never stopped, and spoke over his shoulder. "Since we've acknowledged a certain chemistry between us, it would help if you avoided making double entendres."

Given that his back was to her, she didn't need to hide the surprised parting of her lips. She hadn't meant the phrase to have a double meaning, it'd just popped out. She'd pulled a tiger's tail and she'd need to be more careful from now on. "Point taken."

Seth started the engine and busied himself with things that were totally unfamiliar to her. When she'd been playing the piano, ordering from room service or working the television remote in her suite—things she must have done before she lost her memory—she'd instinctively known what to do. But the yacht was foreign, with its chrome rails, shiny white surfaces and towering mast. She wasn't a sailor, then.

She gravitated to where Seth stood behind a polished wood wheel. "Can I do something?"

After waving a signal to Jai, who released the rope at the front, then the one at the back, Seth spared her a quick glance. "Can you sail?"

"I don't think so," she said, looking around again. "Nothing here is familiar."

Seth frowned. "So we don't know if you get seasick, either. I didn't think about you not knowing."

Seasick? Her mouth dried. She tried hard to see if her body remembered being seasick in the past, but no luck. If it remembered, it wasn't sharing the knowledge with her brain. She could only think of one source for this information. "My mother would know, but asking would have defeated the purpose of the trip."

They reversed slowly away from the dock and then turned toward the open sea. Seth kept a wary eye on her as he maneuvered the vessel. "How are you feeling now?" he asked when he'd raised the sails and the hotel was growing smaller.

She closed her eyes for a moment, felt the motion of the yacht, but no nausea or unease registered. "I'm probably fine. But perhaps we should avoid large swells and not test the theory."

"We're not going that far." He adjusted their course and she saw they were heading north, following the coastline. "There's a place I used to go to have time alone when I was younger. A little bay—no one around, and calm water, so you should be fine on the way and when we're motionless."

"Sounds perfect." It really did. But…if they were isolated, and Seth kissed her again the way he had on the piano, would she have the strength to stop him? Or would that brazen woman who'd pulled him closer emerge again to take control? Her pulse spiked, and she pulled her shawl around her shoulders and wrapped it tight.

Resisting the urge to watch Seth, she sat on one of the cushioned seats and looked out from under the canopy at the night sky. Stars twinkled in an inky blackness and a curved moon shone down. Her hair was back in a braid, but escaping tendrils fluttered around her face in the breeze created by the yacht's movement. She closed her eyes and soaked up the feeling of being out here, away from land, away from people's expectations. It felt like…freedom.

Their direction changed again and she opened her eyes to see a bay up ahead. A rocky shoreline was topped with silhouetted trees, silent and stark. They pulled into the bay and Seth released the sails, stilling them on the water that seemed phosphorescent in the yacht's light.

"What do you think?" he asked from the wheel.

"It's magical." She stepped out to the softly lit deck at the front and turned in a slow circle, admiring their spot from all angles—until she came back to face Seth, the most stunning view of all.

He smiled, and it was only a small movement of his mouth, but it said so much, as if he was pleased she liked something that was personal to him. Then the expression was gone. "Jai prepared dinner. Would you like to eat first or have a glass of Champagne?"

Suddenly hungry, she grinned. "Both."

A strong breeze blew his shirt against his torso, outlining shapes that her fingers wanted to trace, and he rubbed at his chest absently. "Why don't you have a look downstairs at what he packed while I drop anchor and get us sorted."

She went down the little stairway and found a whole other world. Wood-paneled cupboards and counters, broad lights in the ceiling, and compact dining furniture—all so welcoming and cozy. She spotted the picnic basket and peeped inside. There was enough to keep them fed for a week, but it was the chocolate-coated strawberries that she pulled out to have with the French Champagne she'd spied in the ice bucket. Listening to the rattle of the anchor being dropped, she packed everything she needed into the picnic basket, climbed the stairs, and laid the rug at the flat spot near the front of the deck.

A few minutes later, she knew Seth had come up behind her by the outbreak of goose bumps across her skin. She turned and thrust the Champagne bottle into his hands, almost as a defense. "Would you like to open it?" she asked nervously.

"Sure." He took the bottle and removed the cork with only a small sound, and without losing the cork. From everything she'd seen of him so far, the action was vintage Seth—the job accomplished with minimal fuss and an efficiency of action. She allowed herself a small smile.

He filled the flutes and handed her one. "Here's to my plan to satisfy us both."

Before he could clink their glasses, she pulled hers back. "It was your idea to avoid double entendres."

"Very true." He cocked his head to the side, and she couldn't tell if he'd said it on purpose or not. Or which option she'd prefer. Then he raised his glass again. "How about, 'here's to finding a solution that's fair to us both'?"

"Better." She touched her glass to his, the intimacy reminding her of when their lips had touched, and she shivered.

"Not really," he said, his mouth curving into a lazy smile, "but it'll do."

April sipped her Champagne, watching him over the rim of her glass. Watching him watch her with those navy blue eyes that taunted her dreams. Her face warmed and she hoped her blush would be hidden by the night's shadows.

Breaking eye contact, she reached for the dish of strawberries and held it out to him. He took one and slid it into his mouth, eyes not leaving hers as he chewed. She swallowed hard and turned to the railing to gulp some fresh air. It didn't clear her mind.

Every part of her felt him as he came to stand beside her, his back to the view, leaning on the railing. "April, I'm tired of fighting this." His voice was impossibly deep.

Surely he hadn't meant that how it sounded? That they should let their attraction take its natural course? Her hands trembled and she sipped the sparkling contents of her glass to cover. "You agreed."

He moved close. Too close. "I was a fool."

"You had reasons," she said on a cracked whisper.

Taking her Champagne glass, he put both down on the deck before standing behind her and drawing her back against his chest, arms around her, his hands linked and resting low on her belly. "I can't even remember the reasons," he whispered against her hair.

Body molded into his, the feel of him pressed along her almost wiped logic from her mind. But she had to try. "I have reasons."

His hands ran down her sides, shaping her, and the heat of his mouth rested against her ear. "I dare you to name them."

And then he took her earlobe between his lips, tugging, licking, and she didn't want to fight it anymore, either. She'd spent far too much energy since she'd met him trying to deny her body's demand for him, trying to ignore the passion he roused in her. She turned, winding her arms up around his neck.

His arms pulled tight, and the hardness of his chest against her breasts, his arousal against her stomach, made her ache for him all the more.

"April," he murmured between intoxicating kisses along her jawline, "you've been driving me crazy."

The intimacy of his words, of his husky voice, sent a tremor through her. "Crazy?" she managed to say. "You're too sane, too controlled for that."

"I left sanity behind days ago. I've barely been able to think of anything but you." He nipped gently at her bottom lip. "Wanting to taste you again. Not being able to have you."

Her knees sagged and she leaned into him. "It's been the same for me."

"Then let's stop fighting it." Fingertips stroked along her side in the lightest of caresses, sneaking around to just under her breast, not touching the sensitive flesh, but so close that her nipples tightened and a sound suspiciously like a purr escaped her throat.

Oh, the lure of him, enticing her into a state of breathless abandon. It would be so easy to let go. But she summoned the strength to deny him. To deny herself. "We can't, Seth. I've remembered those reasons."

"Are they strong enough to withstand this?" His mouth claimed hers with a possession that made her sway on her feet. Fortunately, one of his hands cradled her head and the other pressed her flush against him, securely holding her. His lips moved confidently, his tongue exquisitely possessive, tormenting her. Inside she was melting into a delirium of desire.

Then he pulled back bare inches, leaving them both

panting into the night air. "So tell me—can you remember those reasons?"

Reasons? The fog in her brain gradually cleared and she recalled what they'd been talking about. And her decision not to get involved with the man she was locked in a battle with over the hotel. Or *anyone* until she remembered who she was.

Though that had been a dream of a kiss….

She sighed, then reluctantly replied, "Only just. But yes."

"Tell me," he said, voice seductive. "Prove to me that you remember."

She took a moment trying to form words around the thoughts in her mind. "All I know about myself is from some reports you had made, and a couple of weeks of memories. How can I take this step, get physically involved with someone, when I don't know who I am?"

"Fair enough." He rested his forehead against hers. "Okay then. Just give me a moment to catch my breath. To convince my body that we're stopping."

His chest pressed against hers every time he drew in lungfuls of air. Then he stepped back in slow, deliberate movements and leaned against a thick wire that led to the mast. "What other food did Jai pack?"

She almost took a step to follow him, to stay in the circle of his heat, but caught herself in time. She could do this. Summoning a tremulous smile, she knelt to the picnic basket. "There are some sandwiches," she said as she pulled the gourmet creations out, "and some salad sticks." She retrieved the skewers threaded through cherry tomatoes, olives, cubes of cucumber and capsicum.

Still breathing unevenly, he said, "We need to talk about something neutral for a moment. I'd ask you about your childhood or places you've visited on tour, but you haven't remembered anything along those lines, have you?"

There was no baiting in his eyes, no test, and it was as if the moon and stars suddenly shone brighter. "You believe me?"

"Yes," he said without hesitation. "I have a fairly good idea of your character now. You wouldn't lie about something like this."

She didn't reply. Couldn't. This small gesture of approval and respect shouldn't matter so much, shouldn't make her heart take wing, but it did, and in that moment she didn't try to examine why, she just smiled and basked in the feeling.

Seth lowered himself to the rug, with an arm's distance between them. "So I guess that rules out you entertaining me with stories and anecdotes."

Her smile faded. "I'm starting to worry my memory will never come back." It was a fear she hadn't let herself form into words before.

"It will," he said simply.

"But what if it doesn't?" She lay back on the rug, looking at the stars above, as if they could give guidance. "Can I go through the rest of my life not remembering? Relying on media reports and my mother's descriptions of everything I've been through, everything I've experienced?"

"If that happened, we'd find more information." He stretched out beside her, mirroring her pose, and laced his fingers behind his head. "You wouldn't have to rely on one person's account."

The way he so smoothly inserted himself into her future, making contingency plans for her benefit, made her want to smile, but she restrained it. Being pleased by his respect was one thing, factoring him into her future was another.

As soon as the hotel issue was sorted, they'd be going their separate ways.

Instead, she let her mind drift along a path she'd mentally traversed often during her walks on the grounds. She turned her head to see him watching the stars. "Don't you think memories are part of what makes us who we are? What if our personalities, our *selves* are the sum total of everything that's happened to us, how we've reacted, the choices we've made?"

When he didn't reply, she listened to the sounds of a never-silent ocean until he spoke, lulled by the gentle rocking of the creaking boat.

He drew up one knee, the rug beneath them snagging with the motion. "There might be some truth in that, but I believe we're born with certain characteristics, perhaps inherited, perhaps our own. I know that in personality, I seem to have more in common with my half brother, Ryder, than I did with Jesse. Yet Jesse and I had more experiences in common."

She considered this, mentally tested it against her theory, exhilarated to be discussing something real, something conceptual. She rolled on her side to face him. "You and Ryder are both an eldest or an only child. Jesse was a youngest, and that would probably affect his experiences more."

"True," he said, still staring above. "You know, I've never thought about Ryder and I having anything in common, besides our father, before. But we're both determined, both competitive."

"Both leaders," she added. "Both men of action and honor."

Tilting his head toward her, he quirked an eyebrow. "You know this *how?*"

"I know you fairly well now," she said, repeating his

words from earlier. "And I've been reading the papers in the past few days. There's been quite a bit of discussion about your family and its history." Which she'd devoured with an eager curiosity. "Ryder's been there a lot. Most stories are covering his engagement to Macy Ashley and buying her father's company."

"And her father's company's stock in our company," he said with a knowing glint in his eye.

The instinct to tread warily warred with a burning desire to know, to understand this man and what drove him a little better. She drew a breath then took a chance. "What does that mean for you?"

He neither shrugged off her question nor bristled at her interest, but seemed to take it seriously. "Ryder and I both have equal shares in Bramson Holdings, with the balance held by several others."

She remembered the name from the report he'd given her a few days ago at breakfast, and from the frequent mentions in the media. "That's the company that owns the hotels."

He nodded. "It's a parent company. Our father inherited it from his father and spent most of his life building it up. It was a food conglomerate when he inherited it, made up of smaller companies manufacturing products such as frozen meals, sauces and the like."

She tapped an index finger against her lips. "So why go into hotels? That's quite a leap."

"When Jesse and I were young, I think he realized he wouldn't be able to train us in the same business he was training Ryder in. So he diversified. He wanted something very different."

The idea surprised her. From what Seth had told her about his father and his two families, and from what she'd gleaned from the papers about the man and his lifestyle, she hadn't formed a favorable opinion of Warner Bramson. But having the two companies, wanting to do the right thing by all three sons, was unexpectedly sensitive.

She reached for the Champagne glasses they'd put aside earlier and passed one to him. "But why not have completely separate companies? Then he could have left the food businesses to Ryder and the hotels to you and Jesse."

"Good question." He sat up a little to take a sip of his Champagne. "I'd always assumed he would. But instead, his will split his majority share in the entire company between us. Ryder got half, and Jesse and I shared the other half."

So the father hadn't split it evenly between all three sons? Instead, he'd pitted Ryder and Seth against each other with his will—not quite as sensitive. "Did Jesse leave his shares to you?"

"Jesse didn't have a will," he said, voice solemn. "He was never very organized. But since we owned the shares jointly, they automatically came to me. Everything else he had—which wasn't much—went to our mother. Which means Ryder and I then had equal shares. But without a majority, neither of us can take control of the board of directors."

Still on her side and resting up on one elbow, she took a mouthful of the sweet Champagne, finding herself intrigued by the story. And the man telling it. "And now he has more shares than you, after buying his fiancée's family business?"

"Yes," he said with a slight grimace.

"Enough to have a majority in his own right?"

A trace of a satisfied smile danced at the edges of his mouth. "Still not quite enough. But I'm sure he's working on purchasing more stock as we lie here."

"And you're not?" She took the last mouthful of

the Champagne and set her glass down near the picnic basket.

His shoulders squared. "I've chosen a different path."

"You've been building alliances," she said in a moment of insight.

"Yes." He finished his glass as well, but instead of putting it down, he turned it by the stem, examining it from all angles, before finally setting it aside. "Ryder won't get a majority share—the other shareholders won't sell. I'm planning that they'll vote in a block with me when it comes time."

And she didn't for a second doubt he'd achieve it. "But you'll always have a hostile brother on the board. He'll be furious that you won, and constantly trying to undermine you."

His chin lifted to a dignified angle. "Nothing I can't handle."

"Will it be worth it?" She could think of nothing worse than being locked into a situation of conflict with no way out.

Seth rolled over onto his back and laced his hands behind his head again. "It will be worth it."

That sounded like Seth—his eye was on the goal, knowing that he'd be able to handle whatever came afterward.

"Perhaps it was good there were only three of you," she murmured.

"According to *some,* there were only three of us," he said, then after a moment he added, "A man called JT Hartley has crawled out of the woodwork, claiming to also be Warner's son."

She watched him carefully for signs of what this meant to him. "You might have another half brother."

"A claimant to the will," he corrected. "I'll handle that, too."

She lay on her back again, and looked up at the same stars, listening to the water lapping against the hull, the occasional little splash of a fish in the distance.

Seth pointed up into the black sky. "When I was a child, I used to wish on that star at night."

As she turned to look at him, the picture before her of his masculine beauty against the majestic night sky backdrop was so perfect it almost hurt her eyes. She looked away. "What did you wish for?"

"The usual. A bike or new baseball glove. That my mother wouldn't cry when my father visited his other family." His voice turned hard, betraying an age of pain, and her heart cracked open for the little boy he'd been.

"She did that in front of you?" she asked in a rough whisper.

A smile that didn't reach his eyes slid across his face, as if to downplay the effects of his childhood. "She'd probably be horrified if she realized I'd known. Jesse was oblivious, but I always knew. It was a good lesson, though. One I'll never forget."

"Lesson?" She had to stop herself from drawing back, almost afraid to hear the answer.

His gaze remained on the stars as he spoke. "Nothing good ever comes from love or commitment."

She studied his tense profile. Such a cold worldview. Then one thought leapt out at her—Seth had never been someone's first choice. His father had chosen Ryder to be the publicly acknowledged son. His mother had chosen to wait around for his father over finding a more emotionally secure environment for her sons. How had that damaged him deep down?

"Surely," she gently challenged, "sometimes, love and commitment can work?"

"It doesn't make people happy." His voice was flat, almost as if this was a mantra he'd said to himself before. "It doesn't add anything to their lives. I've always wondered why people are so desperate for it."

She swallowed the gasp back before it escaped her throat. "You really believe that?"

"I've never seen any evidence to prove otherwise."

Not knowing what else to say or do to ease the pain of the child still living in his heart, she scooted a bit closer. "Show me which star."

He pointed again and she followed the direction. "That's Vega," she said.

Eyes trained on her face, he rolled on his side, bringing him within inches. "You *know* that?"

"Yes. I'm not sure how, but yes, I *do* know." A thrill of discovery raced through her bloodstream and she pointed to another one. "And that's Altair, and Deneb over there. They form a triangle with Vega." Her heart lifted, began to sing at finding another part of herself.

Ignoring the path her finger traced over the constellation, he watched her—she knew it by the gooseflesh that erupted across her skin.

"Which other stars do you know?" he asked, voice deep.

"That's Venus over there," she rushed to say, pretending it was only the revelations of her memory that were heating her skin. "Which, of course, isn't a star, but it's sometimes been called the evening star, or morning star, depending on where it's at in its cycle."

Strands of hair that had escaped her braid danced around her face and he smoothed them back and tucked them behind her ear. "What else, star girl?"

Cheek still tingling from the touch of his hand, she looked up into his eyes, sparkling and intense, and so much more beautiful than stars in the sky. "I don't know any others," she lied.

His eyes darkened; his voice became rough. "Tell me something else then. Something you do know."

The slow burn she'd been trying to forget flared to life, demanding her attention and threatening to engulf her. "I know how I feel when you look at me that way."

"How?" He was closer, his breath grazing her skin, his scent surrounding her, keeping her spellbound.

Throat parched, she swallowed hard before she could speak. "Like the world has melted away, and the only thing that's important is that you keep looking at me."

"I'm not looking anywhere else."

Pulse beating like a herd of stampeding elephants, her gaze flicked to his mouth, wanting it, wanting him. "And that I might die if you don't kiss me."

"Well, I wouldn't want to have your death on my conscience, would I?" he said as he leaned closer.

Seven

When Seth's mouth touched hers in the lightest of kisses, April didn't fight it—the time for resisting him had passed—her body's insistent yearning for this man was inescapable. As she lay in his arms, she accepted the tenderness he offered and parted her lips, asking for more. Yet he kept the kisses chaste, brushing gently, tracing the bow of her top lip.

He cupped her face in his palm, and a shiver broke out, low and deep inside. "Seth, make love to me," she whispered.

For endless moments, he didn't reply, just stroked the hair back from her forehead and pressed his lips to the skin he revealed. "I can't."

With the pulse of arousal strong through her body, she closed the inches that separated them, pressing herself along the length of him. "Yes you can."

His hands gripped her shoulders tightly and he squeezed

his eyes closed, as if gathering himself. "You have reasons not to."

Even rough with restraint, his voice stirred everything inside her, awoke every cell. "I've forgotten them," she said.

"I had reasons." He ground the words out, as if part of him would rather deny them.

She reached to stroke the stubbled surface of his cheek. "I don't think you remember them, either."

"Jesse," he said with haunted eyes.

Suddenly cold, she dropped her hand. He was right—neither of them knew if she'd been involved with his brother.

As she started to move away, he held her in place, his features taut, eyes squeezed shut. "Crazy thing is, I just don't care anymore if you were seeing Jesse. It means nothing."

She stilled, then tucked the wisps of hair caught in the light breeze behind her ears and leaned back into him. "For what it's worth, I'm ninety-nine percent sure I wasn't. I feel, somewhere deep inside, that I wasn't involved with him."

"Even better," he said as he expelled a long breath, then kissed the line of her jaw.

A moan that began deep in her throat escaped. "Then make love to me."

"No," he said as he pulled the strap of her dress down her shoulder and kissed the exposed flesh.

"Is this about the hotel?" She reached to pull his shirt up, to touch his skin, but he laid a staying hand over hers.

"No, I've solved that." Hand still holding down on hers, his lips seared at the hollow of her throat.

Every touch of his lips and hands evoked sensations that made her writhe in his arms. She should ask how he'd resolved the hotel issue, but she was too far gone with sensation. Later—she'd ask later. "Then why?"

"Because you won't thank me for it in the morning." His voice was a rough whisper, and deadly serious.

That was all? A corner of her mouth quirked in a smile. That was easily fixed—she just needed to prove she was onboard with this plan. She guided his face a little lower, in the direction of her aching breasts. "That's my problem."

His heart hammered steadily against her stomach, yet he resisted her guidance, gently nipping the skin where the slope of her breast began. "You said no to the same suggestion earlier. I might be ruthless in business, but I'd like to think I'm a gentleman."

"Seth," she said, slowly going out of her mind, "if you weren't a gentleman you'd have taken me an hour ago."

His cheek rested against her chest as it rose and fell with her breaths. "A big part of me wanted to seduce you into changing your mind an hour ago."

"I've changed it now." Craving his hands all over her, she curled a leg around his hard thigh, hoping he'd understand how close to the edge she already was.

He sucked a breath between his teeth. "That's just the moonlight," he said, voice strained, "the water at night, the swaying of the boat."

Snaking her hand down to his groin, she found him hot and pulsing. "It's wanting you."

He groaned and took her mouth once more, pushing himself against her palm. "Ask me again," he said, his breath mingling with hers.

She held his face with her hands, waited till he met her eyes, wanting him to know she was serious, too, that this was what she wanted. "Seth, make love to me."

"Heaven help me," he rasped, and his mouth came crashing down on hers. Rocking his hips against her, he dragged the top of her dress down, taking the edge of her bra with it, and his tongue swept over the beaded peak of her breast. Tugging her nipple with his lips, he molded the other with his hand and her back arched, her pulse chaotic.

She lifted her legs and wrapped them loosely around his hips, feeling the hard, erotic pressure of his erection against her stomach, reveling in it. Hungry for it. Hungry for him.

Abandoning the top of her dress, he lifted it off from the skirt instead, revealing her thighs and stomach to the night air. Then his hands were sliding over the powder-blue satin and lace of her bra. Her nipples budded tightly, wanting his mouth back there. She wriggled, trying to remove the dress completely, until Seth caught on and stripped it off over her head. In almost the same instant, his hot mouth traced her breast through the lace.

The sensations he was creating with his mouth, with his hands on her other breast, filled her entire body with a blissful turbulence and she was helpless to do more than bask. She looked up into the velvety night sky, sprinkled with thousands of pinpoints of light. It would be impossible to find a more majestic backdrop for the glory Seth was stirring within her, the fire and the frenzy.

"Look at me, star girl," he said, his eyes brighter and more alluring than any of the stars above.

"Why?" she teased, though her ragged breath ruined the effect.

His hands skimmed around her waist, embracing her with his burning palms and fingers. "Because I can reward you better than anything out there can."

"Really?" She threaded her trembling fingers through his hair. "Show me what you've got."

His eyes flashed with challenge, even as his hand slid

down over her belly and feathered over the junction between her thighs, eliciting a gasp from her lips. Then again, lightly over the satin, and a third time. When his hand retreated, her hips lifted to follow, and his gaze sought hers, his eyes wickedly triumphant.

"Okay," she rasped. "Another point made."

"I thought you might see it that way," he said, and then gently bit down into the soft flesh of her breast. She sucked in a breath and ran her hands up under his shirt until she found his bare skin, and scraped the tips of her nails over the warm, smooth flesh of his back, exhilarated when he shivered. The scent of his skin filled her head until her senses swam. He swiped his shirt over his head and she took her fingernails south, over the ridges of his abdomen, and he rolled to the side a fraction to accommodate her.

Letting her nails still trail their path, she leaned to whisper in his ear, "Tell me something."

"At this moment—anything," he said, his voice bordering on pained.

Her nerves were raw with wanting, making talking difficult, but she had to ask, "Is that your only trick?"

He raised an eyebrow as he drew a rasping breath. "Think you can handle more?"

"Try me." Anticipation shimmered along her thighs, her arms, her body. His eyes were full of the devil as he slowly scraped the pads of his fingers along the sensitive skin of her inner thighs, so slowly that she had trouble catching her breath. When his fingers reached the top, eyes still locked on hers, he ran a knuckle down the front of her panties. A whimper escaped her throat.

"Okay," she managed to whisper. "You have my attention."

"I'll keep it, too," he said as he edged his fingers under the fabric and repeated the stroke, this time with a fingertip, and this time, flesh touching flesh. She melted into the rug below her, limp and wretched. Why had she denied herself this—him—for so long?

After slipping off her sandals, his shoes followed. Then he tugged his trousers off. Freed of the restraints, she pressed close, only the thin fabric barrier of her panties and his boxers separated them. Her mouth closed over the naked skin of his shoulder, tasting the masculine blend of saltiness and musk.

Keeping most of his weight on his forearms on either side of her, he lowered his head to her throat, nuzzling and sucking the sensitive skin he found there. She couldn't restrain a gasp—his mouth was hot and wet and exerting exactly the right pressure. She'd *never* get enough of him.

Her hands roamed to his biceps, gently squeezed their firmness, and desire for him made her light-headed. "Seth," she said, not even able to form the words to tell him how much she needed him.

"I know," he said, seeming to understand. With a growl, he lowered his weight to her. She allowed herself long moments to wallow in the feel of his heaviness bearing down on her, the crisp hair of his chest rasping against her sensitized breasts, before she wriggled out from under him. She wanted *everything*. She pulled his boxer shorts down and threw them aside with a little too much effort. They both watched the underwear go over the side and fall into the water.

With a depraved glint in his eye, Seth turned back, pulled down her panties and sent them over the side to join his. All she cared about was that the barriers were finally gone—she couldn't waste a precious second's thought for her underwear, with him naked and ready above her. She arched her hips up to him, her muscles convulsing with need. "Now, Seth."

He reached for his trousers and within less than a minute he was above her again, fully sheathed. And then he entered her with a firm, fluid stroke and she gasped his name, consumed by the intensity of having him inside her, where she'd wanted him so long. He stroked once, experimentally, then whispered, "April," on a ragged breath, and thrust again.

The beauty of his lovemaking, the sheer rawness of it, enslaved her, bound her both to him and the thrusting rhythm they created together. She wound her ankles behind his buttocks, wanting as much as she could take from him, arching up and pressing close.

He moved faster, harder, and the volatility of her need rose, microspasms of ecstasy only whetting her appetite for what else he could bring.

Beyond speech, her hands stroked over his back, his shoulders, feeling the flex and release of his muscles, wanting more, everything he had to offer, praying the moment would never end, desperate for release. And then the moon and the constellations above converged into one exploding sun behind her eyes, sending pulsations of light and pleasure to every cell in her body, and Seth convulsed in her arms, following her, and she was in outer space with Seth and the stars, weightless, grasping his shoulders as her anchor, trying to catch her breath.

Secure in his arms, she lay beside him for what seemed like hours, feeling the gentle roll of the yacht with the water's motion. She could have stayed all night, but as her body cooled, the air on her skin became cold and a shiver rippled across her arms. Seth grabbed the corner of the rug they lay on and tugged it across them, creating a cocoon.

He nuzzled her cheek, leaving a kiss on her cheekbone but then pulled back, looking at her with a quizzical expression.

"What is it?" she asked.

He leaned up on an elbow to look down on her, his eyes sparkling. "I've just thought of something."

"Tell me." She smiled dreamily up at him.

He cocked his head to the side, taking his time. "You don't remember anything before the day you met me."

"True," she acknowledged, trying to see where he was taking this.

"So—" he placed a kiss on the tip of her nose "—you don't remember being with any other man."

"No." Not that she wanted to be thinking of any other man when she had this prime specimen stretched out beside her.

"In many ways, this is your first time." He arched an eyebrow, looking like the cat with the cream. "I'm your first lover."

She stilled as she took his meaning. He *was* the only man she remembered making love with. "Is that a problem?"

"I like it," he said with a wicked grin. "If you don't regain your memory, I'll always be your first."

She chuckled. "I don't think tonight will fade, no matter what."

"I hope not." He leaned down and kissed her again, long and slow; then when they pulled apart, he asked lazily, "Can you reach the picnic basket?"

Popping a hand from beneath the rug, she reached out experimentally. "Yes."

"Did we leave any of those strawberries with the chocolate?"

"There were a few I didn't put out in the dish." She lifted

the lid and felt inside for the container they'd been in, and pulled it out. "Four."

Seth stretched, feeling very content with the world. He smiled at April as she handed him the strawberries and thought he'd rather have her again than the food. But they still hadn't gotten down to discussing the reason for coming tonight, so he'd wait. There would be time to love her body again. Something that spectacular deserved an encore. Or seven.

He took the container, took out one ripe, red berry with a thick chocolate coating over its bottom half, and fed it to her, before eating one himself.

"I'm so glad I came to Queensport—thank you for making it possible," she said dreamily. "I love it here."

Rubbing his fingertips up and down her arm, he placed a kiss on her shoulder and smiled. She'd like his plan, they could resolve this matter of the hotel and then make love again before returning. "I know. That's why I worked out a solution to our situation with the hotel."

"I'm listening." Large eyes that reflected the moonlight gazed at him and he felt the pull to lean into her again, but stopped himself.

He cleared his throat. "The Lighthouse Hotel has personal significance for you—it's where you first sang in public with your father. I understand that." And he did understand, especially after seeing her reaction to the video. "But I need the hotel back before the board members find out and decide I don't have secure enough hands to control all of Bramson Holdings."

"And I understand that," she said with an earnestness that was endearing.

He lifted her hand and interlaced their fingers, pleased they had some common ground with their appreciation of each other's needs. "But you don't require the entire hotel—you need access to the grounds, and a place that's permanently yours."

"What are you suggesting?" Her eyebrows swooped down in concentration.

"We draw up a new contract, to give you ownerlike rights to one of the presidential suites. You can live in it, or use it for holidays—much like owning a serviced apartment in a luxury resort. In addition, the piano is yours. I've already had the staff move it to your suite while we're out here tonight. It has personal significance for you, and the Lighthouse Hotel can just buy another instrument."

"And in exchange?" she asked, wariness creeping into her voice.

"You sign the papers declaring your agreement with Jesse is null and void. You'll keep your house with its recording studio, as well as your recording label. You end up with everything."

"Except the actual hotel, which you keep along with the confidence of your board members," she said slowly.

"Exactly." He smiled, pleased with his solution.

She pulled the rug tighter around her. "What if I want the *actual* hotel?"

His chest deflated a little. On first explanation, she didn't like the plan, and that was a shame, but it was still a good deal for her.

He gently rubbed her shoulders where the tension had built. "My preliminary legal advice indicates that if this goes to court, you'll lose. You'd be left with only what you started with. This way, you come out ahead—owner's rights to one of our best suites, the piano, plus everything that already belonged to you."

Her hands covered his and stopped his impromptu massage. "You said you now believe that I've lost my memory."

"I do." Confused at the change of direction, he pulled her hands down under the warmth of the rug, between them, and waited.

"Then you'll see that I can't accept your offer." Her voice held an edge of pique. "I'm not giving away my claim on the hotel until I've remembered why I wanted it in the first place."

"April," he said gently, "you need to be reasonable. We have no idea how long your memory will take to return. I can't have this hanging over the company's head indefinitely."

"What if I wanted it for more than somewhere to visit? I won't know until I remember."

Suddenly weary, he closed his eyes and rubbed a finger across his forehead. Was it unreasonable to want this resolved? "And what if you never get your memory back? Perhaps you need to start living in the present."

The only part of her that moved was her eyes as they widened. "That's your plan then. It's time for me to give up on regaining the parts of me that are locked away in my brain somewhere. And take your offer."

He shoved a hand through his hair. "That's not what—"

"And this," she said, flinging an arm out toward the picnic basket, the yacht, the stars, "this was your inducement to start living in the present? Make love to me and butter me up so I'll accept your grand solution?"

"That's not what happened between us tonight and you know it," he said through clenched teeth, entire body tense.

The air around him became heavier, bitter, making it difficult to breathe. He knew she wouldn't believe that when she'd calmed down, but her accusation just proved he should never have given in to his baser desires and taken her tonight. She grappled for her clothing and began to pull it on under the rug, so he stood and let her have the whole blanket to work with. He found his trousers and yanked them on, then his shirt, tugging it around his shoulders.

When she was dressed, she stood at the guardrail, her back to him, but her voice carried clearly on the night air. "I do know you weren't using me."

Her admission did nothing to soothe his anger, given the anger was aimed squarely at himself. They'd crossed a line. A line he should never have let them get near. "Perhaps we both went too far tonight."

"Perhaps we did," she said, looking up at the stars. Then she turned and her gaze settled on him. "I'd like to go back now, please."

Anger drained away at the sight of her stricken eyes, leaving only the hollowness of regret in its wake. He nodded and headed for the console, noticing that she packed up the leftovers from their picnic and folded the rug before sitting on the cushioned bench seat and gripping the rail beside her with a white-knuckled fist.

He raised the anchor and, not bothering with the sails, started the engine, then turned the yacht for home. Several hours too late.

Eight

Seth sat across from April and her mother in the hotel's restaurant, wondering why he was putting himself through this torment. One week had passed since he'd made love to April on the yacht, and yet, here he sat, engaging in small talk over lunch, pretending he wasn't physically restraining himself from reaching for her and holding her sweet body flush against his once more. But he would never let himself reach for her again—that night under the stars had proved that some lines should never be crossed. He wanted his hotel back from this woman. That was all.

He'd been working long hours from his suite and meeting April and her mother at mealtimes, except for the one day he'd made a trip back to his office in Manhattan. It was still his original plan to keep an eye on her, wait for the moment her memory returned so he could reclaim the Lighthouse Hotel. But sometimes, in the dark of night, when sleep wouldn't come, he wondered how honest he was being with himself, and if it was April herself keeping him here.

But that was ridiculous. Hanging around to be near a woman was not something he'd ever do. It was the type of behavior he'd have expected from Jesse, not himself. He vowed long ago to be a fool for no woman, and staying here, just to see her, definitely qualified as foolish.

He glanced across at her, radiant in a simple cinnamon-tone dress, and his pulse spiked. His physical desire for her was another thing. But he wouldn't let that make a fool of him, either.

"Darling," her mother said sharply, "how is your quiche? Mine has too much salt. And they've been atrociously spare with the asparagus. Do you remember the asparagus and pine nut quiche we had at that little restaurant in Paris a couple of years ago? Simply divine."

April winced. "No," she said quietly, eyes haunted.

Seth clenched his jaw. Was her mother trying to spark a memory, or was she just insensitive? He cleared his throat and changed the subject. "Have you had a chance to listen to the CDs?"

He'd ordered April's entire backlist and had them shipped here, and had thrown in all the DVDs of her live concerts that were available.

Light suddenly filled April's beautiful eyes. "I've been meaning to thank you for them. When I hear the music, I can remember the words and melodies, and can play most of them on the piano."

After her refusal of his plan a week ago, she'd tried to return the piano to the ballroom, but he'd already ordered another one, so he told her to keep it. Besides, he liked to know she was playing it, to hear her music float in through their interconnecting door.

Her mother sipped her martini. "Oh, yes, she's been playing them constantly."

Seth raised an eyebrow. "Surely you think that's a good thing? Anything April remembers brings her a step closer to regaining her full memory."

He'd done some research on the internet, placed a couple of calls to specialists. Seemed there was no way of predicting how long someone's memory would take to return—or any guarantee that it would. But April's snippets of memories, like the names of stars in the constellations, were apparently a positive sign, and he had full confidence she'd make a one hundred percent recovery, and soon.

"Of course it's a good thing," her mother said, all sweetness and smiles. "But she could be listening to them just as easily at home, where she has several pianos. Much easier all around."

Easier for her, Seth silently amended. He'd also done more digging on the mother. As April's manager, she took a fifteen percent cut of everything her daughter earned. It wasn't unheard of in the entertainment industry for a family member to be a manager, especially when the artist had become famous as a child, but he had to wonder how it impacted on the current situation, on her insistence on getting April home—where Mrs. Fairchild would have more control. And on signing his document to regain the recording studio and label and forfeit the hotel. If April suddenly became a hotel owner instead of a jazz singer, then where did that leave Mommy Manager?

Not that he wanted April to keep the hotel. No, he wanted her to sign that document to rescind the earlier contract as soon as possible. But it felt somehow sleazy to be on the same side as Mrs. Fairchild.

Repressing a shiver of aversion, he turned to April. "I'm glad the CDs are helping."

"It's funny," she said, as if to herself, "my memories of events, days and people might have abandoned me, but the music is still there."

The winsome effect of her faraway eyes and her hair falling to partially curtain her face was almost too much for him to bear—his breathing became uneven, his arms ached with the need to hold her close.

From the corner of his eye, he saw Mrs. Fairchild glaring at them, radiating disapproval. "Darling," she said, feigning interest in her lunch, but in actuality, still watching them both like a hawk, "I had a truly puzzling call from Emerson earlier."

April's face was blank—she didn't know who the man was. But Seth did. He had a small pile of phone messages from Emerson Scott that he had no intention of returning.

"Oh, come now," her mother said. "Surely you remember *Emerson?*"

April showed no extra comprehension after her mother's helpful emphasis on the name. She'd just told them that she remembered no one, and her mother shouldn't have needed the reminder anyway. Wherever this was going, he had a feeling deep in his gut he wouldn't like it.

"Emerson?" April said, looking from him to her mother.

"Emerson Scott." He almost snarled the name. "Movie actor. Celebrity." Pretty boy. Renowned ladies' man.

April's forehead puckered the way it did when she was trying to force her memory. "I'm sorry, the name doesn't mean anything to me."

Her mother shook her bracelets farther down her wrist. "Well, that surprises me. You're practically engaged!"

A roar of denial rose in Seth's chest, but he held it in

check by clenching his fists till they felt as if they'd snap. The claim was impossible.

April's eyes flew to his, and he could read the thoughts there—if she was engaged, then their explosive passion on the yacht was wrong. She'd been unfaithful. But the idea of April belonging to another man was intolerable, and he refused to believe it.

The mother was lying.

He pinned the older woman with his harshest stare. "Explain *'practically'* engaged."

"They've been together forever, and *everyone* knows they'll marry one day. I wouldn't be surprised if they already have an understanding between them." She tittered a laugh and cut another dainty slice of her quiche.

"Oh," April said, eyes downcast. She put her cutlery beside her plate and folded her hands in her lap. "What was puzzling about his call earlier?"

"He's excessively worried about you—you're quite the center of his life! But he can't get through on the phone, so he rang me to check and to ask you to call him."

Seth held his breath when April looked at him, her eyes asking if he'd been fielding calls on this front. Of course he was—he'd told her he was intercepting her calls, and the last thing she needed in her vulnerable state was a skirt chaser.

He gave a slight nod. Her eyes widened then turned to ice. Her mother, with what he was sure was premeditated timing, chose that moment to turn in her chair and call for a waiter and order another martini, giving them a small slice of privacy.

April leaned over and whispered close to his ear. "You blocked calls from my boyfriend, *then* seduced me?" Two spots of color rose on the apples of her cheeks and restrained anger vibrated in her voice. "Knowing I was involved with someone else. And not even telling me about the other man."

She leaned away again before he replied, but that was fine—she wasn't the one to clear this up. Gut churning, he turned his attention to the mother. "It seems strange to me that a man who is 'practically' engaged to a woman wouldn't have visited her in hospital after a major road accident."

Mrs. Fairchild waved away his question. "He was in Prague, filming his latest action movie."

"And," Seth continued, "hasn't found a way to check on April, besides ringing her mother four weeks later." One thing he knew for a fact—if he'd been the man engaged to April, no one and nothing would have stood in his way to his fiancée for four weeks, let alone after a well-publicized car accident. In fact, he couldn't believe it of any man. He pulled out his phone and connected to the internet.

Mrs. Fairchild patted her daughter's hand before picking up her martini. "Emerson is a busy man, but we all know how much he cares."

April obviously picked up on the anomaly, too. "Have I ever told you that I'm going to marry Emerson Scott?"

"Not in as many words," her mother said carefully.

Target located, Seth handed April his phone, displaying images from gossip magazines of her supposed fiancé with his arm around a starlet. April scoured the photo. "He seems attached to this girl."

Her mother leaned over to see the screen then shrugged. "Actors are affectionate people. It means nothing."

But his April was a smart woman; he could see her doing the math, putting the clues together. His chest expanded with pride as he watched her square her shoulders and turn to the older woman.

"Mother, have I told you I was even dating him?"

With a wave of a matchstick-thin arm, Mrs. Fairchild dismissed the need for confirmation. "You didn't have to, darling. A mother knows."

"Have you ever—" April's eyes narrowed "—seen me kiss him or be affectionate?"

Her mother's mouth opened like a stunned fish. "You? You don't kiss men in front of people. You won't even touch them. You're just not the sort of girl to be passionate about anything besides your music."

Seth leaned back in his chair with a thud. The woman who'd kissed him to within an inch of his life while sitting on a piano with his entire staff on the other side of the door? The woman who'd made love with him in the open air on the yacht? Nothing in this conversation was making sense.

He called a waiter over. "Go to reception," he said too quietly for the others at the table to hear. "Tell them to find the number Emerson Scott left in his messages. Get them to ring him, tell him Seth Kentrell is ready to return his calls, and bring the phone to me."

"It's okay," Mrs. Fairchild was saying as he tuned back into the conversation at the table, "we can visit him tomorrow. He's in New York at the moment. We can pack up this afternoon and leave in the morning."

April appeared to have changed tack and was eating her side salad, perhaps in the hope her mother would drop the subject. He could help with that.

The waiter reappeared with the phone and Seth pressed it to his ear. "Mr. Scott?"

"Yes," a voice came back, deep and smooth. Too smooth. Seth's hackles rose.

"This is Seth Kentrell." He met April's widened eyes and held them. "You rang the Lighthouse Hotel some days ago."

The other man cleared his throat. "I was looking for April Fairchild."

"April is here, but she's recovering from her accident." Still holding her gaze, he gave her a slight nod of reassurance. "Can I ask the nature of your relationship?"

His voice warmed. "April and I are old friends."

Seth raised his eyebrows at April, but she frowned back at him, clearly impatient for the information. He couldn't restrain a smile of anticipation as he said, "I was under the impression you were practically engaged."

Emerson spluttered out a laugh. "Engaged? Where did you hear that—was it in the papers? Oh, Lord, if it's in the papers please don't let Brandi see it," he ended almost under his breath, as if sending up a prayer.

The mountain of tension that had been sitting on Seth's shoulders dissolved and he thumbed the speaker button so April and her mother could hear for themselves. "So you really are just friends with April."

"Why? What did she tell you?" the other man asked, confusion clear in his voice. "Hey, did you put me on speaker?"

Seth's eyes flicked to Mrs. Fairchild, who was picking at her food, pretending not to be listening in. "The engagement story didn't come from April," he said, smoothly avoiding the last question.

"I wouldn't have thought so. We've been friends since we were children. Famous fourteen-year-olds who understood each other's lives. Listen, I just need to know she's okay."

"She's okay. I'm sure she'll call you soon." He hung up the phone and handed it back to the waiter who'd been watching from a distance. Then, with the world set to rights again, he turned to April. "You're not engaged. Or dating. It seems there's someone called Brandi who would have a problem with that scenario."

"Thank you," April said on a long breath.

Her mother raised her eyes to the ceiling and exclaimed, "If you would just sign the contract, April, we could leave."

"I'd like to know what you were playing at—" April began.

"It's *just* a place you stayed at when you were a child," her mother interrupted, her tone shrill. "We know that. Give the nice man his hotel back, and let's get home so you can find your memory around the things that are truly familiar, and you can pick up your career again."

April flinched, but her voice didn't waver. "I'm not leaving yet."

Having no intention of hearing this argument again, Seth changed the subject. "April, tomorrow my brother Ryder and his *fiancée*—" his subtle emphasis on the word seemed lost on Mrs. Fairchild "—are arriving. I need to speak to him. Would you like to meet them for brunch with me and help Macy stave off certain boredom while Ryder and I talk about the company?"

Macy Ashley was reputed to be a rising star in the business world. It was enough that Seth had agreed to meet his half brother again to talk about the new claimant to their father's will, he didn't need a "rising star" muddying the waters by trying to impress her fiancé.

The older woman smiled in her sickly sweet way. "Darling, if we leave in the morning, you won't—"

"Mother, *I'm* not leaving. And your pushing isn't helping." Then, in an elegant motion, April angled around to face him. "I'd love to meet your brother and his fiancée. Call my room when you need me." Then, head held high, April stood, picked up her shawl and sailed from the room.

Her mother turned to him, eyes blazing like an avenging demon. "I know what you're doing."

"Do you?" he asked, casually reclining back in his seat.

"You're using my daughter." She grasped her purse, her spider fingers clutching it tightly on her lap.

He stiffened, but casually cocked his head to one side. "Tell me what you're using your daughter for, Mrs. Fairchild. If she honestly wants this hotel, why are you trying to talk her out of it? How much do you stand to lose if her recording career ends?"

"And how are we different, Mr. Kentrell?" She spat the words at him. "You want the hotel. That's your own self-interest, yet you're pretending to be friendly with her."

A growl built in his throat but he restrained it, unwilling to lose his temper with anyone, least of all this woman. "April is easy to be friendly with."

"And if I'm not mistaken, you want something more from her now. Again, it's self-interest, but my daughter is not a loose woman, Mr. Kentrell, and I won't let you take advantage of her."

"Good to know," he said, beyond caring that his sarcasm would be lost on her.

She stood, looking down on him, grasping her purse to her chest. "I might want to be comfortably kept, but at least I'm not taking a lecherous route to get there."

She stalked off, leaving Seth reeling. Her dart had hit its mark.

Seth sat at his makeshift desk, returning an email to the Bramson Holdings' head of public relations. No one would be in the PR unit now—it had passed midnight some time ago—but he couldn't sleep. Better to be working than to go to bed and toss and turn, replaying the loop of memories featuring April lying naked under him on the yacht. Of her warm, moist mouth kissing him like there was nothing or no one in the world she wanted more. Of her breasts filling his hands, their peaks pressing against his palms.

He looked down at the email he'd been typing and couldn't remember what it was about. *Damn,* he had to stop doing this. He squeezed his eyes shut and held the bridge of his nose. After a few minutes of trying to focus, he realized a faint melody floated on the air, lifting his soul.

April.

His legs moved of their own volition, taking him to the connecting door between their suites—the place he listened whenever she played. Tonight, as with most nights, it was a slow, haunting piece of music, unfamiliar and achingly beautiful.

His body tightened and demanded the perfect fit of hers as his hand moved to the doorknob, but he didn't turn the handle. Instead, he leaned his back against the door, lungs laboring, and rested his head on the hardwood behind him. He couldn't risk walking through to her suite—no question it would lead to the out-of-control passion they'd experienced the first time he'd listened to her play in the ballroom. The passion that had finally been consummated on the yacht.

She'd rejected his compromise—the plan he'd devised to suit them both, leaving them free to explore the passion. If she had just agreed, their business dealings would be over now and they'd be just two people with a crazy chemistry. He could walk through this door this minute and bring her back to his bed. But she'd said no, and until the hotel issue was resolved, his career was at stake. It wasn't a time to let down his guard.

The music grew to a crescendo, enveloping him, pulling at him, and although it took every ounce of his willpower to do it, he resisted. Then her voice joined the instrument and the words were of wanting. Of aching and sadness. And more wanting. A cold sweat broke over his skin and his hands trembled with the effort of restraining them from flinging open the door and going to her, losing himself inside her.

Then an insane thought struck—what if he didn't hold back, just for tonight? Allowed himself to take the woman he craved to his bed? He turned the doorknob a fraction, but the music stopped and the last notes faded away. He paused. Had she seen the handle and known he was there? Or had the piece simply ended?

Insatiable need clawing at him, he waited. The music didn't start again, and after about ten minutes he finally conceded she'd finished for the night. Probably gone to bed. Lying there now, maybe naked, her long limbs sprawled across rumpled sheets, her hair covering the pillow, her curves begging him….

Swearing, he tore his hand away and strode back to his laptop. *Work.* He needed to focus on work and his career. Not on a woman who would be gone from his life soon.

He was playing a long game, and he couldn't afford to take his eyes off the ball.

With restless fingers, April smoothed down her dress and knocked on the interconnecting door to Seth's suite. She hadn't been sure what to wear for this meeting with Seth's brother and his fiancée, and had sorted through the clothes that her mother had sent ahead when she left hospital. A soft, flowing, below-the-knee dress in navy blue had seemed best—maybe because the color reminded her of Seth's eyes—and she'd slipped it on with some tan, strappy sandals.

The door swung open and Seth stood there, gorgeous in a white business shirt, the top few buttons undone, and dark trousers. The dark hair peeping from the V at his neck robbed her mouth of moisture.

He opened his lips to say something but the words didn't come. Instead, his eyes traveled a path, from her loose hair down her length, coming to rest on her toes peeping through the sandals, leaving a trail of fire where his gaze had touched.

Heart thumping an uneven rhythm, she fidgeted with the skirt and looked down at herself. "Is this okay for the meeting? I wasn't sure…" Her voice trailed off. Seth had been helping her since they'd arrived—for his own interests, sure, but he'd still been helping her. This was the first time she would be helping *him* with something, and she wanted to get it right.

He swallowed hard, his Adam's apple bobbing. "You look good." He stood back to let her through the doorway.

The simple compliment brought warmth to her face, so she took a breath and focused on her role. "What do I need to know about today?"

His hands reached for his collar, twisting sideways as he fastened the top buttons. "I'd rather you didn't mention the situation with the hotel. Until it's resolved, my half brother doesn't need to know."

"And if we *resolve* this by you keeping it, he'll never know?" she asked sweetly.

Hands dropping to his sides, he grinned, acknowledging her point. "Something like that."

"Okay, no mention of the contract." She relaxed a fraction. Being on the same team as Seth felt…nice. "How do we explain us being here then? And our relationship?"

"I'll tell him you're an old friend of the family, and I'm staying close by during your recuperation."

"An old friend? Surely he'll realize something is wrong

there. He will never have heard my name associated with yours before."

He disappeared through a doorway to one of the bedrooms, and part of her wanted to follow, to see the bed she'd been imagining, but then he appeared again, a red tie with a gold pinstripe in hand. "Ryder Bramson knows nothing of my family. Besides, your injuries came from an accident involving Jesse. It's not an illogical leap to us having known each other, as well."

"Okay, no mention of the hotel, and I'm an old friend of the family." She watched him tie a Windsor knot, mesmerized by his deft hands, the skin of his throat, wanting to touch both. She shook her head and forced herself to refocus. "What about the amnesia? Will I try to hide it?"

"That one is your call." He slid the knot into place and straightened the tie while watching her.

Explaining to strangers could make her feel vulnerable—she liked the arrangements Seth had made here at the hotel that meant she didn't have to tell anyone. But then again, if they didn't know, she'd have to bluff any personal questions, which may or may not work.

"I'll play it by ear," she decided. "Is there anything you want me to specifically do with Ryder's fiancée?"

"Macy." He grabbed a jacket from the back of a chair and slipped his arms through the sleeves. "She's been working for him and seems to be something of a rising star. She may want to listen in."

April felt a moment's uncertainty. Macy was a business-woman. With a memory. Ryder would be more ably supported in this meeting. She glanced at Seth, shoulders broad in the jacket, feet shoulder width apart, looking like a victor already—he'd succeed without the extra support, but even so, she'd like to offer what she could.

"Do you mind if Macy wants to listen?"

Seth stopped, resting his hands low on his hips. "It'll depend on how their relationship has settled."

She replayed his words in her head, but they still didn't make sense. "Settled?"

He shrugged. "I mentioned that when Ryder became engaged to Macy, he acquired her father's ten percent stock in Bramson Holdings. Just when there's going to be a battle for control of the board, he's strengthened his position through a marriage. I don't believe in coincidence. He was marrying her for the stock. Therefore, I don't know what kind of relationship they have, whether he shares anything with her."

April wrapped a hand around her throat. How sad, to get married for such mercenary reasons. And what did this say about Seth—did the mercenary bent run in the family? His tone hadn't been disapproving over his brother's actions, or troubled at the waste. Would he go as far as Ryder to gain control of their company? She shivered.

But her role here wasn't to judge him. It was to help him. Though she still wasn't sure how, exactly. When he'd invited her, he'd said it was to help Macy stave off boredom. She realized now that the truth was somewhat different—he'd probably been reluctant to talk details in front of her mother.

She tucked her hair behind her ears. "So what do you want me to do?"

"If Ryder lets her listen, then it probably means he would have told her afterward anyway, so it can't hurt. But I don't want her interference in the conversation. This will be the first business discussion I've had with my half brother, and we don't need intrusion."

"So, again, I'll play it by ear," she said as he grabbed his wallet, key card and a shiny silver pen.

"Yes." He walked to the main door. "And, April, thank you for doing this."

"I just hope I can be of use."

He paused and put a heavy hand on her shoulder, looking deep into her eyes. "You'll be great."

She dragged in a breath and nodded, then they walked down the corridor toward the elevator. "I don't need the elevator anymore, if you'd prefer to take the stairs."

He cast her an assessing gaze. "Are you sure?"

"I'm building my strength." Taking the advice of the physical therapist at the hospital, she'd purposely been using the stairs and avoiding shortcuts, now that she was up to it.

"Good for you," he said approvingly, and they headed for the stairs.

As they reached the lobby, she looked around. She'd been so focused on what to say and wear that she hadn't thought about where they were going. "Where are you meeting them?"

Seth smiled at Oscar, the hotel's manager, as he passed them. "I had a marquee put up out on the grass. The staff erects them for events and weddings."

They stepped out of the lobby and she saw the high canopy in the distance, with food-laden tables and four chairs. A gentle breeze fluttered the edges of the snow-white marquee and the clothes of the two people standing beneath it.

"It's lovely." She exhaled, imagining a beautiful wedding or joyous celebration held in just that spot. "But you didn't want a formal room?"

He looked down at her, his eyes of darkest blue, hard and unwavering. This was no celebration—he was going to war. "I wanted to guarantee privacy from staff. And I couldn't bring myself to invite Ryder to my own suite. This seemed like a good compromise."

"It's perfect."

They approached, and the couple came to the edge of the shaded area, tightly clasping each other's hands. The man's rugged features were as closed as Seth's, but the woman had warm, hazel eyes and April instantly liked her.

Seth put out his hand to his brother. "Ryder, thanks for traveling out here for our meeting."

Ryder shook his hand. "No trouble. I've been wanting to take Macy away for a few days, so we'll drive on and head for Cape Cod."

Seth turned to Macy and smiled with more warmth. "I'm pleased to meet you." He put a hand to April's back. "This is April Fairchild. I invited her to have brunch with us."

Without releasing Ryder's fingers, Macy reached for April's hand. "I'm glad you could come along. And I have to say, I was sorry to hear about your accident. Ryder and I both love your music, especially your *Live From London* album."

Unsure how to respond to such a specific compliment, April hesitated, stomach clenched. Then she felt Seth's hand at the small of her back pull her a little closer and she knew she could face this.

She smiled. "Thank you, Macy. Unfortunately, you're more familiar with my backlist than I am. You see, I lost my memory in the accident."

Macy's face transformed into complete sympathy. "I'm so sorry to hear that."

"I'm sorry to hear that, too," Ryder's voice rumbled. "And Seth is looking after you?" Ryder was watching them with mild curiosity.

Seth pulled her another fraction of an inch closer,

tension radiating from his body. "April is an old friend of the family. She's spending some time here to recuperate, and I'm keeping an eye on her until she feels stronger."

Ryder's face didn't change but Macy smiled. "I'm glad you have someone you can trust."

April's stomach dipped. There was that word again—*trust.*

Seth moved toward the chairs. "Would you like to take a seat? The staff have outdone themselves putting on a brunch spread for us."

They all moved and took seats along a rectangular table—Macy and Ryder on one side, and Seth and April on the other. The brothers were directly across from one another and April had the sense of two caged lions circling. Each of them took a plate and began to fill it with food.

Seth spoke as he took a pastry from a platter. "What have you found out about this JT Hartley?"

Ryder shrugged. "Probably the same as you. He's in property development. Came from the wrong side of the tracks, brought up by a single mother. Snagged a scholarship to Yale and started building his fortune soon after graduation."

Seth offered April a tray of small cakes as he replied to Ryder. "His mother once worked in a secretarial pool at Bramson Holdings. We can't find out if she ever had direct contact with Warner, but it's unlikely. She worked seven floors down from his office."

April nibbled on an apple cupcake, feeling very out of place hearing this privileged information. She'd imagined that she and Macy might leave once the conversation got down to business. Then she realized something that made her stop chewing. Seth trusted her. She'd often wondered whether she could trust *him,* but having her sit in on this meeting showed his faith in her discretion and judgment.

A smile danced around her lips, so she took another bite of cake to conceal it.

Ryder poured Macy a cup of tea, then himself a cup of coffee from a pot. When he handed it to her, a look passed between them that lasted less than a second but held a world of affection, respect and love. Seth was wrong. Ryder and Macy were a love match.

Ryder turned back to his half brother. "I had a call from Pia Baxter, the executor, on the way out this morning. Hartley's attorney is asking for a DNA sample from both of us to prove his client's paternity."

Seth made no effort to hide his contempt for the request. "He can ask. I'm not helping his claim."

Ryder nodded. "He's obviously confident if he's asking for DNA."

"I have to admit," Seth said, sitting back in his chair, resting an arm along the back of April's, "I didn't believe him at first. But maybe Warner did have an affair before he married your mother or before he met mine. Of course it's more feasible that his mother has spun him a tale. Otherwise, why now? Why not come forward when Warner was still alive?"

Ryder finished chewing a mouthful before replying. "Unless he did and Warner sent him packing."

"Frankly," Seth said, leaning forward, "even if he's got the right DNA, I have no intention of splitting this company further. Warner had every chance during JT Hartley's thirty-seven years to include him in a will, and he didn't."

Blinking slowly, Ryder subjected Seth to a lazy assessment. "What do you propose?"

Seth met his half brother's gaze head-on. "We take a united stand. We can't fight battles on two fronts at the same time, run the company, and expect to win everywhere."

Ryder's brow rose. "What would a united stand entail?"

"We call a truce in our roles at Bramson Holdings and the board in the short term. Until the JT Hartley problem is resolved. We fight him together. Then we resolve the rest between ourselves."

Ryder sat back and folded his arms over his chest. "You think we can work together in a truce?"

One corner of Seth's mouth turned up. "As I said, short term. We have a handshake deal, agree to the terms and then the entire deal is voided when Hartley walks away empty-handed."

Nodding slowly, Ryder unraveled his arms. "I could work with that. But—" he cocked an eyebrow "—I'll still win Bramson Holdings once our deal is voided."

Seth chuckled. "Good luck with that." Then his face sobered and his voice became forged steel. "But this fight is between you and me, always was. I won't tolerate a new player on the scene who thinks he can stake a claim to something we've worked for since we were teenagers. I don't care who he thinks his father was—I have too much invested."

April froze inside. This Seth was a different man than the one she'd come to know—except, perhaps, the version of him she'd met in the hospital room. How could he be this ruthless, this cold-blooded toward a man who may prove to be his brother? Something in her chest shriveled and died.

"Agreed," Ryder said.

Seth pulled a legal pad from the end of the table and took the silver pen from his pocket. "Let's talk terms."

Nine

Macy's chair scraped back as she stood. "April, I'd love to see the little beach over there, if you could show me."

"Of course," April said, collecting herself. She'd been transfixed, following the negotiations between the brothers—her world shaking as she watched the transformation of Seth into a cold-blooded businessman—and had forgotten the role he'd brought her to play. Seth slid her a quick smile of approval and she returned a more tentative one before leaving with Macy.

Macy chatted casually about the scenery until they reached a small patch of sand that met the water between the more rocky land edges. "I'm sorry if I dragged you away, but your face lost its color and you looked like you could do with some air."

April's stomach swooped. Had her horror been written on her face? Had Seth seen it? She drew a shaky breath and said, "Thank you."

Macy slipped off her shoes and sat on the knee-high, grassy embankment that edged the beach. April followed suit, wiggling her toes in the cool sand. "I guess I'm just a little tired."

The light breeze toyed with Macy's hair and she tucked some wayward strands behind her ears. "I can't begin to imagine what you're going through. You must feel so lost. Is there anything I can do?"

"I don't think anyone can help, but I appreciate the offer." April looked over at Seth talking to his brother and silently acknowledged that, despite her assertion to Macy, Seth had been instrumental in recovering the few memories she'd regained—he'd provided the information on her background that had helped her remember her father, then had found the videotape that had given her back her musical knowledge. And he'd made her stay at the hotel possible that had prompted flashes of déjà vu, which was surely bringing her closer to remembering everything. For his help, she'd be forever grateful.

How could she feel so many conflicting emotions about one man?

She turned back to the other woman and shrugged. "I just need to remember."

"This might seem forward—" Macy kicked a little puff of sand in the air "—especially considering the delicate nature of Ryder and Seth's relationship, but I'll leave you my number. I've been living in Australia and don't really know anyone here anymore, so I could use a friend myself. Though to be frank," she said as a blush stole up her neck, "I've never had too many friends, no matter what country I'm in."

Shoulders relaxing, April began to feel at ease and smiled. The only other person she'd felt comfortable being with since she'd woken was Seth. Although most of their time together probably couldn't be described as "comfortable." Another contradictory emotion she felt about the man.

Still, it was nice to find someone else she could let down her guard with a little. "At least you know what your social situation is," she said. "I might be terrible at making friends—I have no idea."

Macy laughed, a sweet sound, like birdsong. "I somehow doubt that. But seriously, ring me if there's something I can do. Even if it's just to chat."

After plucking a blade of grass, April twirled it between her fingers. "Would you answer a personal question?"

"I'll try."

She'd been watching Ryder and Macy when they all sat down under the marquee, and had been curious about the nature of their relationship. Seth suspected Ryder had clinically proposed to Macy for her stock in Bramson Holdings. But April had seen more between them.

She twirled the blade of grass one more time then released it to the breeze. "You and Ryder," she began, "you seem to be in love."

Macy smiled widely. "Very much. Though I can still hardly believe it."

"Why not?" April tucked her feet underneath the edges of her dress.

"I didn't think we'd make it, not until just recently. I had my own issues, but Ryder…" Macy trailed off, and they both looked back at the brothers, heatedly debating some point of their temporary truce.

April swallowed hard, remembering Seth pushing her to rescind her claim to the hotel—after they'd just made love. "I think perhaps neither of them escaped their childhoods unharmed."

"Seth, too?" Macy asked sympathetically.

April bit down on her lip and nodded, eyes still on the men.

"One thing's for sure," Macy finally said, "their father really did a number on them both. I hope it works out with Seth the way you want."

Works out? April couldn't breathe in past the air trapped in her lungs. Nothing would "work out" between her and Seth, she understood that now like never before. She would be dreaming to consider otherwise—even for a fraction of an instant. Right this minute, Seth was across the lawn, protecting his company from threats. She'd watched him—he'd been merciless, and she couldn't deny *she* was a threat. What was his plan for *her* after she'd rejected his last solution? She was suddenly cold. This was the wrong place to be. With him.

It was time to leave.

As soon as she'd survived today.

She turned to Macy and summoned a smile. "Have you been to New England before?"

Macy looked out to sea and closed her eyes, as if smelling the salty scent on the breeze. "No, I grew up on the West Coast, and I've been in Australia since I was eighteen."

"I don't think I've been to Australia—at least no one's mentioned anything about me going there," April said with a self-deprecating laugh. "Tell me what it's like there."

Macy's voice filled with enthusiasm as she spoke about her adopted country and April listened, fascinated. When Seth and Ryder began to walk across the grass toward them, she was still engrossed, and checking her watch, realized an hour must have passed.

When they came closer, Seth's eyes zeroed in on hers and she held back a quiver of awareness—and the wince as her heart cracked a little further, knowing she'd be leaving him soon.

Continuing as hostess, she and Seth walked their guests back to the hotel's entrance, all engaged in small talk about the scenery and the weather, and waited with them while the valet retrieved Ryder's car. When the valet returned, Ryder held out his hand and Seth took it, and they shook firmly. But both men remained guarded, and April knew the moment they'd dealt with JT Hartley and this truce was cancelled, they'd be lunging for each other's jugulars again. It was sad, but maybe rivalry and mistrust was how it needed to be between them—it was all either would accept from the other. All they would accept from themselves.

Macy and April's goodbye was warmer, but then, they had nothing riding on the outcome of the brothers' battle.

Seth watched them go and then turned to her, face still unreadable, as if he couldn't let go of the role he'd slipped into for the meeting just yet. "Thank you."

"You're welcome." She looked over to the grassy embankment where she'd made a vital decision only an hour ago. "Seth, there's something I need to tell you."

He dug his hands into his pockets. "I have to make a couple of calls to set the new plan into motion. Can it wait fifteen minutes?"

Her belly squirmed at the thought of having to wait until she could say the words aloud, but the cowardly part of her was happy to delay, to scrounge any remaining time here. "Fifteen minutes is fine."

"Where will I meet you?" he asked, glancing inside. His mind was clearly on the Bramson Holdings calls he wanted to make.

April cast her gaze from the ocean to the green lawns to the wilder woods at the edge of the grounds. This would be her last afternoon here and there was one place she wanted to see again.

"I'll be waiting in the lighthouse," she said, and walked away.

April scaled the stairs of the disused lighthouse with a heart heavier than the stone surrounding her, but with only mild strain to her muscles. It was amazing how quickly her body's strength was returning. Would she heal as quickly on the inside? Her memories still hadn't returned, and now she was about to create two new holes inside her—one in the shape of the Lighthouse Hotel and the other in the shape of the man who filled her thoughts and dreams. The man her body craved.

When she reached the glassed-in top, the sparkling ocean stretched into the distance, endless, timeless. It had been there before she was born, and would be there long after she was gone. The time her lost memories covered was insignificant against such a scale, yet they'd caused so much trouble, not only to her, but to her mother, to Seth and to others.

The faint sound of Seth's footfalls growing louder on the concrete steps seemed to create a beat in her mind that echoed the marching of time. Time she was wasting here in this escape from reality. In a fairy tale.

When he came into view from the winding staircase, the beat in her mind became more chaotic to match the spike in her pulse. He was a picture of harsh masculine beauty, with his dark hair ruffled by the breeze outside, his navy blue eyes bright in the reflected light, and the breadth of his shoulders emphasized by their compact surroundings.

How would she be able to tear herself away from him to leave?

He stood in front of her, hands low on his hips. "You had something to tell me?"

"Actually—" she paused, biting down on her lip "—I have something to ask you first."

"Ask," he said, voice deep and solemn.

Crossing her arms under her breasts, she looked up and met his gaze. "Watching you with your brother, talking about your family empire, I realized how important it is to both of you. You'd do anything to protect it, including neutralizing the threat JT Hartley is posing."

He nodded warily. "Of course."

A shiver raced down her spine and Seth slipped his arms from his jacket and wrapped it around her shoulders. Though she hadn't shivered from the cold, his jacket was still warm with his body heat and she couldn't bring herself to give up one of the last connections she'd have to him.

"Thank you," she said and pulled it around her like an embrace, giving her the strength to say what needed to be said. "I'm also a threat you've been trying to neutralize."

Face pained, he glanced from her out to the horizon. "I won't deny that there's pretty much nothing I wouldn't do to secure the hotel."

"I thought so," she whispered past a parched throat.

"But you *know* there's something between us." He turned back to her, eyes fierce. "Don't pretend what you felt in my arms wasn't real."

Even now, heat swirled through her limbs, down low in her belly, and that was merely from his proximity. She knew with one touch he'd have her alight. And the same flammability had been in his eyes from the start. "I won't deny it, but—" she drew in a long breath "—what I can't work out is where that desire ends and 'neutralizing a threat' begins. Do you even know where that line is?"

He closed his eyes and gripped the rail till his knuckles were bloodless. "No, not always," he rasped.

Her shoulders slumped forward, absorbing the blow that she'd known was coming, but which rocked her nonetheless.

"I'm leaving in the morning, Seth," she said as gently as she could, not wanting it to sound like a fit of pique or a punishment. It was just what had to happen. "I should have followed the doctor's suggestion to start with, and gone home to familiar surroundings, but at least I'm doing it now."

His entire being was so tense that he looked ready to fracture. Still gripping the rail, he turned his head to look at her through haunted eyes. "There's no need for you to go."

"Seth—"

A shudder ripped through his body and he looked down at his hands on the rail as he cut her off. "You're right. You should go. I'll regret saying this later, but you should go."

It took everything she had not to go to him, to ease the tension in his features, in his shoulders. To ease her own pain.

Instead, she took the smallest of steps back. "I'll stay in touch about the hotel, and I promise I'll keep trying to regain my memory."

"I don't doubt it." He smiled, a sad curve of his mouth. "My legal team will let you know of any developments in their work to check the validity of your contract."

"I appreciate it." She removed her arms from the sleeves of his jacket and held it out, but when he reached for it, his hand closed over hers and held.

"Can I offer you one final piece of advice?"

The heat from his palm was close to scorching. She swallowed hard before she could speak. "Of course."

He took the jacket with his other hand, not releasing her fingers, and threw the garment haphazardly over one shoulder. Still clutching her fingers tight, he said, "Take everything your mother says with a grain of salt. I'm afraid her fifteen percent stake in your career is affecting her advice. Just—" he winced, clearly uncomfortable delivering the warning "—be aware."

She gave an awkward, curt nod. Ironically, her mother had told her earlier in the day that Seth wasn't to be trusted, something he'd now confirmed. At least he'd admitted as much, and she respected his honesty.

One thing was sure—*everyone* had their own agenda, something they wanted from her. Her chest constricted painfully. She was truly on her own.

Seth scrubbed his fingers through his hair, leaving it rumpled, but he didn't seem to notice or care. "When will you go?"

"In the morning," she said, her voice breaking. She paused to gain control before continuing, "I'll tell Mom when I go back inside, and then pack tonight to get an early start tomorrow."

"I wish you well, April," he whispered, then pulled her to him. She could barely breathe, but she held him as fiercely, before breaking away and running back down the stairs.

She had to get away. Before he saw her cry.

Seth gripped the Scotch glass tightly, knowing that if he squeezed it any harder it might shatter. The sliding door to his balcony was ajar, allowing the cold night breeze to waft in, along with the notes from the piano in the adjoining suite and April's voice singing about being crazy. Her balcony door must have also been open, giving him an almost ringside seat for the haunting melody.

At one in the morning, he should be asleep. But this was the last night he'd be so close to her, the last time he'd hear her play in these unguarded moments. He couldn't bring himself to miss a second.

He still couldn't believe he'd had the strength to let her go. Up in the lighthouse, he'd been preparing the words in his mind to convince her to stay until her memory returned, until they had the hotel ownership resolved. But then he'd realized he shouldn't. Simply couldn't make her stay any longer when she needed to go. He cared about her too much.

Do you even know where desire ends and neutralizing a threat begins? She'd been right—he'd lost sight of that line long ago. And April deserved better. He'd win the hotel, but not like that.

He downed the rest of the Scotch in one gulp, welcoming the burn in his throat since his entire body was already alight. He'd barely touched her since the night they'd made love on the yacht, and his body was in a constant state of protest. Needing to bring his scorching temperature down, he unbuttoned his shirt, and rolled up the sleeves. She was driving him to distraction.

He squeezed his eyes shut, as if that could block out his insatiable need. It didn't work. He poured himself a second drink and, barefoot, strode over the carpet to the interconnecting door, leaned on it, sipping at his Scotch.

Her voice, so husky yet pure, tore through to his soul, and she was singing about being crazy for someone. Was it just a song? Or was she in the seventh level of hell along with him? Before he could resist the urge, his hand went to the doorknob and he turned it. The door swung open to expose her in a soft caramel nightdress, her hair loose about her shoulders. Beads of sweat broke out across his forehead and his lungs strained to draw oxygen. Her gaze lifted and sparked as it met his over the baby grand, her fingers and voice not faltering from the song, as she sang the words straight to him. His heart hammered an erratic beat; his skin was too tight, as if he'd burst free of it at any moment.

In between lines of a verse about being lonesome and wanting, her pink tongue emerged to moisten lush lips and he was undone. He covered the ground between them in less than an instant, slammed the glass down on the surface of the piano, and drew her from the stool and into his arms. Every muscle tensed to the screaming point, his mouth came down on hers with a crushing intensity that he was helpless to control, but she met and matched him with equal force.

His hands ironed down her sides, catching her nightdress and gripping it in his fists. "One night, April," he said with desperation against her hair. "Give us one last night."

Nails digging into his arms through his shirt, her breath panted near his ear. "I couldn't turn you away now if I wanted to."

In one fluid motion he whipped the nightdress over her head, leaving her naked before him. It was almost too much to bear. He closed his eyes, trying to slow down, then opened them again and looked his fill of her creamy skin. Trembling hands roamed down, savoring the slope of her breasts, the curve of her hips, her round buttocks. He claimed the slick depths of her mouth again, heard a moan and wasn't sure who'd made the sound.

She slid her fingers over the cotton covering his shoulders, leaving a path of fireworks in her wake, and dislodged the shirt down his arms to the floor.

"Touch me," he said on a ragged breath. "I need your hands on me."

She did, oh God, she did—over his torso, the electrical current zipping right through to his bones.

Then she stilled and gazed deep into his eyes. "You're the only lover I remember, but no one else..." She pressed a heated kiss to his pec. "It couldn't be like *this* with anyone else."

She was right. He had all his memories, and it had never been like this with anyone else for him, either. There was something elemental—primal—between them. He grabbed her waist and lifted her onto the shiny black top of the baby grand. "I've never had so little control," he rasped. "It's you. You drive me to the brink."

She was so high on the piano that when he stood between her thighs, he laid his head between her breasts, cradling a luscious globe with a palm, relishing the feel of being so close again. Then he pulled her head down to kiss her, dragging her full bottom lip into his mouth, their breaths mingling.

Her urgent fingers darted for his belt and zipper, but she was too high to reach them, and a small sound of protest came from deep in her throat. He understood her frustration—he needed her hands on him again, touching him. He brought her palms to his shoulders, then grabbed his trousers on either side of the zipper and yanked. The button flew up into the air, and the sound of it bouncing off the lacquered surface of the piano made April's mouth slacken then curve at one corner. "Impatient," she said.

"Beyond impatient for you," he growled. The rapid rise and fall of her chest made her breasts catch the light as she inhaled, and he watched, mesmerized, before capturing a peak between his lips.

"Yes," she whispered, then used the sides of her feet to

pull at his trousers, pushing them to the floor. He snagged
the stool with an ankle and dragged it over, knelt and gained
enough leverage to lean her back, draping the baby grand,
her luscious body a banquet before him, her hair spread
like a halo around her face. Abandoning any possibility
of savoring this slowly, he crawled up onto the piano with
her, covering her body with his own, reveling in the feel
of her softness beneath him.

"Seth," she said, and when her mouth opened to say
more, he took advantage and kissed her, deep and hard.
Her hands slipped beneath his boxers until finally, finally,
she held him, and his entire world contracted to just that
one point of contact. It was too much, but not enough,
nowhere near enough. More, he needed *more*. He shunted
the boxers down his legs, then brought his hands back to
hold her waist, grounding himself with her.

His hand slithered lower, over her hip, gliding over the
sensitive skin of her inner thigh, and she whimpered. The
pads of his fingers scraped again, then higher, until her
breath hitched and she arched her hips, inviting, begging;
and without hesitation, he positioned his knees between
her thighs and thrust forward, entering her, letting her
transport him to the place only she could create, a place
where sensation filled his every cell, where he floated free
of tethers to the material world. A place where her body
belonged to him alone. He pumped faster and her legs
wrapped around his waist, locking at the ankles, urging
him on.

She was near the edge, he could feel it, and her eyes
looked at him without seeing. But he wanted her to
remember this, remember *him*.

"Say my name," he ground out.

"Seth," she said breathlessly, her eyes regaining focus.
"Seth, you're everything."

She convulsed around him, calling his name, and the contractions of her body pulled him over the edge with her, into a place so intense he was in danger of imploding. He shuddered into her, and then he was falling, falling, gripping April, never wanting to let go.

Much later, when he could finally open his eyes, he moved his weight to one side to give her some space, but she murmured, "No," and pulled him back. He tried to balance his weight, not wanting to crush her, but not wanting to be separated, either.

"I've got a better idea," he said next to her ear.

He jumped down from the piano, slid his hands beneath her still flushed body and lifted. She began to protest, but he whispered, "Shhh," and she relaxed back into his arms. She felt so damn right there. He carried her through to her bed and gently laid her on the rumpled sheets before crawling in beside her.

"I'm staying the night," he said, not prepared to argue on this point.

She crawled closer, snuggling against him, and murmured her assent, and within minutes her breathing changed and he felt her go limp.

Sleep didn't come as easily to him. She was so soft, so lush in his arms, and he watched the night gradually fade through the window, dreading the rising of the sun.

Ten

Holding back tears, April sat on the high, grassy ledge that met the sand, watching the choppy ocean under an overcast sky. It would rain later, which seemed appropriate—Mother Nature crying alongside her.

She was ready to go—she'd organized everything last night before Seth had come to her—but her mother hadn't finished packing, so April had said she'd wait out here, using the window of time to say farewell to the only surroundings that were familiar to her. The tears threatened again but she wouldn't let them fall—it was time to face the world, to go to her own home, and she needed all her courage.

From the corner of her eye she saw movement and turned to find Seth walking across the expanse of lawn toward her. As if a sheer curtain had flown across her eyes, she lost focus, leaving the scene fuzzy, so she blinked, then blinked again. Was it Seth? Everything cleared for a second, and she saw his familiar tall shape, his dark hair being rumpled by the breeze. A buzzing sounded in her ears, but it wasn't from her surroundings, it was inside her head.

Suddenly the planet tilted off its axis. Head spinning, she grasped handfuls of grass to steady herself, but everything was slowly revolving about the figure of Seth. Except it wasn't Seth, it was her father, smiling, striding across with his arms held wide, calling her name. The world came crashing down with punishing weight and she choked on a sob.

"April!" Seth's voice was urgent in her ear. His arms encircled her, rocking, but her heart pounded too hard and she couldn't move, couldn't take her eyes from the spot where she'd remembered her father standing, even though he was no longer there. He was gone. *Gone.*

Seth's fingers wiped away hot tears from her cheeks, and he turned her face to his. "April," he said, voice desperate. "What happened?"

Her throat was too dry to speak, and the lump lodged there was too large to even swallow past. Instead, she leaned into him, felt his arms tighten around her, and she held him for dear life. His hands rubbed up and down her arms, as if trying to bring warmth to her limbs, perhaps comfort.

"Tell me you're all right," he quietly demanded.

When she found her voice, it was more of a croak. "I'm fine."

He still held her against him, but she felt some of the tension leave his body. "Then what happened? You looked like death."

She gazed out over the lawn where her father had stood moments ago. Years ago. Her heart clutched as if squeezed by a cold fist. "I've remembered."

With a gentle finger under her chin, he turned her back

to him, his navy blue eyes burning with intensity. "What have you remembered?"

"Everything." A wobbly smile crept across her face as the memories tumbled into her mind. "My father's bear hugs. My childhood dog, Fergus, licking my face. Singing at Madison Square Garden. Giggling with Emerson Scott when we were teenagers. I remember everything."

Past and present slotted into place beside each other, filling her to a nauseating bursting point, but she was secure in Seth's solid arms, safe with him filling her vision.

A sharp voice sounded from nearby. "What have you done to my daughter?"

Seth didn't move, didn't take his eyes from April. "I'll get rid of her," he said quietly.

Despite a shiver crawling over her skin, she laid a palm on his cheek. "Thank you, Saint George, but I need to do this one."

She tried to stand, but her legs were all jelly. In an instant, Seth's arm was back around her waist, pulling her up and against his warm body. She breathed his scent, the same forest-fresh essence that she'd smelled on the first day they'd met in the hospital, when she'd leaned against him much the same way. The desire to melt into him was strong, to let him protect her. But it was time to slay her own dragons, to face down her challenges.

Finding her balance, she took a step away and turned to her mother. "My memory's returned," she said, her voice trembling only a little.

Her mother's face paled, but her chin kicked up. "Then we can finally leave this place for good. We have a lot of plans to put in motion. I'll ring your agent now and ask if he can see us today."

Remembering a lifetime of being steamrolled by this

woman, April squared her shoulders. "No, Mom." Her new life started now, this minute.

"We can talk about it in the car." An overly bright smile stretched across her mother's face like an ill-fitting mask—it was too tight, cracked at the seams. "The valet has it waiting."

April drew in a revitalizing breath. She was the woman she'd been before the accident again, but better. Stronger. In a strange way, not knowing herself for four weeks had allowed her to come to know herself on a deeper level. To rediscover her joy in music and star-gazing and taking time out. Seth was behind her; she could feel the heat he generated. He was ready to support her, but she could do this all on her own. It was past time.

Spine straight, she spoke with the quiet power she could feel inside. "I fired Gerald the day of the accident. We won't be meeting with him today or any day. But you knew that."

"That was a strange time, darling." Her face contorted into a sympathetic expression that didn't match her eyes. "Gerald didn't take you seriously. Let's wait until you're feeling better and we'll talk again."

"I remember *everything,* Mother." April hadn't just told her she was going to fire Gerald—she'd shared all her plans for the future.

Seth moved up beside her, a light hand rubbing the small of her back. "What is it?"

She kept her eyes on her mother as she answered him. "I quit music—recording, concerts, my label. I fired my agent, who pressured me to stay even after I'd talked of needing to step back. Therefore, I no longer have a need for a manager."

There was a pause where no one spoke or moved, the

only sounds the wind whipping along the shoreline and a lone seabird.

"You fired your mother," Seth eventually said, his voice neutral, but holding a world of understanding.

"Darling, you were burned out." Her mother's false smile was still in place, but her voice was becoming more desperate. "We'll go back to your house and you can finish your recovery there."

"I *am* recovered, and I'm not going with you." April softened her voice. "I'm sorry that your job depends on mine, but I can't stay in a career I no longer want just to keep you employed as my manager. And I would hope that my mother wouldn't want me to."

Deep sadness pulled inside as she faced the knowledge that her mother didn't want the best for her, nor support her choices. But that's what came from blurring the lines between business and personal relationships.

Her mother's eyes slid to Seth and back again. "Let's not talk about this in front of strangers. This is family business."

April sighed. Families were supposed to look out for each other. Have each other's backs. There had been a few people like that in her life: her father, her friend Emerson. Seth. She and Seth might be at cross purposes about the Lighthouse Hotel, but she'd trust him with her life. Or—her stomach lurched—was she in danger of confusing the lines between business and personal with *him,* the way she had over the years with her mother?

With no time to analyze that question now, she folded her arms and met her mother's gaze. "No, it's not family business. It's career business. You've made enough from my career to keep you comfortable, and now it's time to separate. Once we've disentangled our business interests, we can talk about our mother-daughter relationship."

Her mother's smile dropped, leaving something cold and pitiless. "You love the fame. You've always wanted this."

Seth's hand at the small of her back stilled and pressed more firmly. April took the strength he offered and stood taller. "Decisions I made at thirteen shouldn't dictate my entire life. I'm making new decisions, starting now."

A stiffness descended over her mother's features as if she was just realizing this wasn't a whim, that it would really happen. Then she shook her head and said, "Call me when you've come to your senses," before turning sharply and stalking off toward her waiting car.

April's knees buckled and Seth pulled her close against his side, supporting her weight. "Are you sure?" he asked.

Her mother's car drove across the paved reception area and down the winding driveway. "Right now, I'm not sure of anything. But yes, I needed to make that break and stand on my own feet. Take control of my destiny."

His expression barely changed, but there was a trace of something akin to pride in the depths of his eyes. "Do you want to sit down?"

"Maybe." She looked around. There was a couple walking some distance away, and a car had arrived with people now emerging from within. Not much activity, but she already felt vulnerable, and being in anyone's field of vision made it worse. She looked up at him. "I've checked out of my suite."

"We'll go back to mine till you decide what you want to do." Arm firmly around her waist, he led her back to the hotel and along the corridors to his room. Blindly she followed, glad he was there to hand the reins to while she needed him.

Shivering uncontrollably, she held him tighter. Once inside, he guided her into his bedroom and tucked her in his bed, under the covers, fully clothed. She sank back into the pillows and, scarcely blinking, watched him as he rang the concierge and arranged for the bags they'd taken from her mother's car to be brought up to his suite.

Then he lifted the covers and climbed in beside her, sitting up against the headboard, and held her face to his chest, stroking her hair. Needing his strength, she snuggled in, wanting the oblivion that his presence normally granted. Instead, her mind raced over past events, putting the scraps she'd remembered in the past weeks into context. Seth murmured soothing words and her eyes drifted shut as she allowed herself to be cared for in this little cocoon from the world.

The shivering gradually eased, and after what seemed like hours, she stretched her legs and looked up at him. "Thank you." Though she was leaving, and he wouldn't be part of her future, there was no one else she wanted here with her in this moment. No one she'd feel as safe with in her emotionally bare state.

"I'm glad I was here," he said, voice low, then he dragged in an impossibly deep breath. "April, don't answer this if you don't want to—" he hesitated and she knew what he was going to ask "—but you said you remember firing your agent on the day of the accident?"

Everything inside her clenched tight. It was time to face the worst of her returned memories—for herself and for Seth. She laid her head against his chest again and nodded, his crisp shirt sliding with the movement. "And I remember the drive with Jesse."

"If you'd rather not…" His voice was strained.

She reached over and took his hand, interlacing their fingers. "I'll tell you." She closed her eyes, frowning, as she recalled the events leading up to his brother's death. "He drove us to the lawyer's office. It was a lawyer he knew out of the city, who'd fitted us in on short notice to write up the contract."

"Why not come to me? Why do it at all?" he asked, face contorted with stifled grief and confusion.

She ran her fingers absently along the front of his shirt. "From what he said, I think he'd never considered himself cut out for the hotel business. He wanted something more glamorous, perhaps something more exciting."

Seth's chest rose under her cheek, held a moment, then dipped with his heavy exhalation. "That sounds like him."

"And I think he wanted to step out from your shadow." She felt him stiffen, and she looked up into his eyes. "He idolized you and felt he could never compete. So he wanted something completely different, completely his own."

"Your recording label," Seth supplied, sounding weary. "Working with musicians and celebrities would give him the glamour and excitement, and in a field separate from me."

"I guess so."

He thudded his head back on the soft headboard. "The fool. Why didn't he *talk* to me about it?"

Although she had no siblings, it wasn't hard to understand how difficult this would be to hear. She shimmied up the bed to sit against the pillows beside him. "That would have defeated the point of doing something on his own," she said softly.

"True." He gave her a resigned smile. "So the lawyer drew up a contract and you both signed it. Then what?"

A prickling sensation spread through her belly, and she pleated the sheet between her fingers. "Jesse had brought Champagne to celebrate his new life direction and he poured us all a glass. I didn't see him drink more than the one glass, or I swear I never would have let him drive."

"The autopsy said he had alcohol in his system, but not much," Seth said, nodding.

She swallowed, trying to moisten her parched throat. "He drove back to the city, and he was talking so fast, lifting his hands to gesture, just so excited."

A smile haunted his eyes but didn't break through on his face. "Jesse was always excitable."

"There were no other cars on the stretch of road, and—and a dog ran out." She flinched, heart galloping, remembering the same flinch when she'd seen the dog as a passenger in the car. "Jesse swerved, missed the dog, and maybe without that touch of alcohol, without his consuming excitement, if both hands had been on the wheel when he saw the dog, he wouldn't have lost control of the car."

She was cold, so cold. He reached for her, pulled her close, tucking her face against his neck. "You don't have to say any more," he said, voice stretched tight.

"I have to." She struggled to make her throat work—the scene was playing out in front of her and she had to get it all out. "I saw the tree. It was coming too fast." She spoke against the warm skin of his neck, tears gathering in her eyes. "Jesse spun the wheel and threw out a hand to push me away, and the driver's door took the brunt. I don't remember the impact," she said on a cracked whisper, unable to stop the tears from streaming down her cheeks. His heart sprinted as fast as hers; she could feel the compounding effect of the beats where their chests pressed together.

"April, you can stop."

His arms tightened around her, making it difficult to draw in air, but she wanted those arms there, holding her in one piece.

Despite the pain in reliving the horror, part of her was glad to be able to give this to him. He deserved the knowledge. She arched back to look him deep in the eyes.

"Seth, his last act was to take the brunt of the impact and protect me."

"Thank you," he rasped, eyes swimming with emotion for the brother he'd never see again, then he pressed a kiss into her hair.

They lay entwined for long minutes, and her pulse gradually slowed, her lungs didn't have to labor to draw breath, and she felt the same easing in Seth's body.

"Tell me how you met him," he said, his voice quiet and low.

She thought back to that fateful night when she'd been so full of optimism about the future and let out a sigh. "We sat beside each other at a dinner party held by a friend we had in common. We both talked about wanting to change careers, and by the end of the night we'd hatched this plan. It seemed like too much of a coincidence to ignore, that we both wanted something new. A perfect opportunity. The second time we met face-to-face was the day we signed the contracts. The day he died."

A sad, ironic smile curved only the very edges of his mouth. "You weren't involved with him after all."

"I barely knew him," she said softly. "You know, I don't have any siblings, but if I did, I think I would have enjoyed a brother like him. He seemed fun."

Seth rolled back, shoulders against the headboard, looking up at the ceiling, but one arm still held her firmly. "He *was* fun, but most of the time I didn't appreciate that about him."

"Families can be hard," she said, thinking of her messy relationship with her mother. But she snuggled in closer to Seth, banishing the problem of what to do about her mother until another day.

"I've lost my father and brother in the space of months," he said with quiet desperation. "There's been too much death." He stroked a fingertip down her cheek. "You're the only thing that feels like life."

The combination of his words and the finger on her cheek sent a quiver through her body. "Until I met you, performing on stage was the most exhilarated I'd felt. But lying in your arms brings me alive like nothing else."

He placed a whisper-soft kiss on one eyelid then the other. "Stay here with me tonight. Delay your return one more night."

There was only one possible answer. "Yes," she said and ran her fingers through his hair, tugging him down.

When his lips touched hers, the intensity of the morning—regaining her memories and telling Seth about his brother's final hours—mingled with her insatiable hunger for him, and the combination was almost unbearably powerful. Their kiss became stronger, hungrier, and she moved sideways to lie on top of his reclining form, the arch in her back making her pelvis press into his. She gloried in the magnificence of the hard masculine body beneath her—he was everything. Everything. She couldn't imagine ever *not* wanting him.

Without breaking the kiss, Seth reached for her thighs, tugging them apart and forward so she straddled him, and the extra pressure against her core almost had her swooning. She bit his bottom lip, urging, giving, *needing*.

Then he wrenched his mouth away and pushed her upright gently. Confused, she blinked her eyes open, but he was already undoing the buttons of her blouse. He drew her back to him, filling his mouth with the side of her breast and the satin fabric that covered it, sucking, gently biting, leaving her helpless to do more than grind her hips against his erection.

He struggled to draw breath as he leaned back against the headboard and held her face firmly in his hands. "I dream about you at night," he said on a rough whisper. The words soaked through her body, resonating with the same truth inside her, and she trembled. She leaned down and pressed her open lips against his, meeting his tongue, sucking it into her mouth.

He rolled her onto her back and slowly, so very slowly, he removed her clothes, piece by piece. And on each new section of skin he uncovered, he placed a kiss. Her heart melted at the beauty of the action and her blood heated with erotic anticipation.

When every last bit of clothing was gone and she lay there naked before him, he smiled into her eyes. "You're perfect. From the top of your head—" he placed an open-mouth kiss on her forehead "—to the tips of your toes…" Hand under her knee, he drew her leg up to kiss the front of her middle toe. "And all the places in between." He settled between her legs, his heavy warm breath feathering across the apex of her thighs.

When he bent and nuzzled, she whimpered. Then his tongue parted her, and she was undone. She cried out his name and writhed beneath his mouth. It was too much—the sensation, that it was Seth causing it. The only thing keeping her anchored was his hands on her hips, holding her in the world. Before she could leave reality entirely, he kissed his way over her belly, up her chest, devoting extra attention to her budded nipples, and she blinked her eyes open, coming back to the present, wanting more.

Rolling to her side, she slithered down the bed and snaked her hand along to grasp him—so hard, yet silky— and a deep sound rumbled in his chest. The intimacy of holding him, of having the power to make him groan, was an addictive aphrodisiac, and she lowered her mouth to take him inside, to take the intimacy a step further and put him completely at her mercy. As she tasted his salty essence, he gasped her name and contorted on the bunched sheets. Smiling, she stroked his ridged abdomen, across the line of dark hair that led to the sensitive skin she kissed.

"Wait," he rasped, then reached for his bedside drawer, and within seconds he'd sheathed himself and rolled above her.

He hovered for endless, excruciating moments, until she said, "Seth, I want you inside me."

His nostrils flared. "I'll never stop wanting you," he ground out. He entered her slowly, but once they were joined, he seemed to be overtaken by the frenzied need that was never far when they touched, and she grasped at his back, bucking her hips, meeting his thrusts, driving them beyond endurance.

When she thought she couldn't take any more, she climbed higher still—higher until she crested the thundering wave, and it crashed over her, leaving her floating in the endless blue abyss. Soon after she felt Seth shudder in her arms and follow, joining her in the abyss, and she sighed because the world was just as it should be.

April lay in Seth's arms, his heart thudding below her ear. She wished the world would go away, that things could be simple and they could just be two people who wanted each other.

But they couldn't.

Because she'd remembered everything, including her plans for her future. And Seth deserved to know.

She stroked his arm, up over his relaxed biceps to his shoulder. His skin, his form, his masculinity was so beautiful. "Seth?"

"Mmm?" he said, and pulled her closer.

"I know why I want the Lighthouse Hotel."

He stilled. "Why's that?"

"Before the accident," she began softly, then found a stronger voice to continue, "I was leaving my recording career. You know I'd already fired my agent and that Jesse's plan seemed like fate knocking on my door. I'd planned to live on the grounds here and be involved in the day-to-day running of the hotel. I could perform at night in the ballroom for guests if I felt like it, but I wouldn't be obliged to."

"Sounds nice," he said, his voice noncommittal.

The vision of that life shone in her mind and filled her with a warm glow. "It's the perfect solution for me. A new career where I can be hands-on and find the pleasure in singing again. If I want to, I can let myself be booked for a concert once a year, or more often if it suits me, but my life would be here. Where my father first invited me onstage. Where I can be myself."

There was an extended moment of silence while she waited for his reaction. Finally he brushed her hair off her face and met her gaze. "Thank you for sharing," he murmured.

She relaxed a fraction and snuggled back down beside him. "I wanted you to understand why I'm fighting for this."

He placed a kiss in her hair and she lost herself in plans and dreams for her new life in Queensport. His breathing gradually changed into the slow, steady breath of sleep but she was too wrapped up in thoughts of her future.

Seth would survive. He'd live on to fight another round with his half brother and struggle for control of the board. Bramson Holdings might even make a go of her recording label—they had the capital to invest and pull in some major stars.

All she wanted was this one hotel. To live here. Work here. Make her life here.

She'd stay this extra night, while he assimilated the information about his brother's death, but she had to go in the morning. Because now that she'd remembered why she wanted the hotel, she was even more determined to fight Seth Kentrell to keep it.

Eleven

Seth lay with April in his arms, feeling totally content. They'd ordered lunch from room service then made love again, and now she dozed, her sated body pressed to his. A lazy smile spread across his face. He could get used to this.

His cell rang from the bedside table and, as he reached for it, April stirred and blinked her eyes open. He gave her a quick kiss on the forehead and thumbed the talk button.

"Kentrell," he said, eyes still on her sleep-rumpled face.

"Mr. Kentrell, it's Angus Jackson."

Giving April a last lingering look, Seth gently extricated himself from her limbs and swung his legs to the floor. He always liked to be alert when he took a call from the head of his legal team. "Go ahead."

"I have some news. We've received further legal advice, and based on that and our own assessments, we're confident that our initial advice concerning the Lighthouse Hotel was correct. The contract between Jesse and April Fairchild won't stand up in court. In fact, I'd be very surprised if it made it as far as court. Jesse didn't have the authority to sign a contract that large on behalf of Bramson Holdings."

A tight coil of tension in his gut began to unwind and he breathed out a sigh of relief. He was safe. As soon as the truce with Ryder was over, he'd be clear to take a run at the chairman of the board. His blood pumped with the electricity of the challenge. "Good work, Angus."

"Would you like me to contact Ms. Fairchild and inform her? Perhaps we can head this off before it begins."

He looked down at April's lush body in his bed. "No need. I'll let her know."

He hung up, but kept the phone in his palm. There were more calls he needed to make—he could finally move forward. But first he needed to tell April. A twinge in his belly made him pause. Losing the hotel would be a blow for her, he knew, but she must be expecting it—he'd told her several times it would end this way. And he'd ease it for her as much as he could.

She was watching him with those large chestnut-brown eyes. "What's wrong?"

Uneasiness clogging his throat, he coughed. "I have some news." He frowned and sat on the edge of the bed. Delivering the detail was surprisingly difficult. Perhaps doing it quickly would be best for both of them, like diving into icy water. "That was my legal team. They've determined that Jesse couldn't act for Bramson Holdings with regards to the document you signed. They've had outside advice, as well." He softened his voice. "April, it won't stand up in court."

"Oh," she said faintly, looking suddenly lost.

If she knew anything about him, she had to know he wouldn't leave her out in the cold. He took her hands and held them together between his. "I know the sentimental value this hotel has for you—I'll arrange something with Oscar so you can come and stay anytime. And the piano is yours. Take it with you."

She blinked and blinked again. Then she withdrew her hands and sat up straighter, regally, clutching the sheet to her chest, face composed. "Thank you for telling me."

Chest expanding, his heart filled with pride. It had been a shock, sure, but his April was an amazing woman. Strong. He liked that about her. "Do you want to order something else from room service? I need to make a few calls."

"I'll be fine." She tilted her head to the phone in his hand. "You make your calls."

Relieved at how well she was taking the news, he brushed a kiss on her cheek, then grabbed his pants and dialed his personal assistant. "Therese, I need you to set up meetings with Anderson, Marx and Seymour for tonight or tomorrow."

"Any time frames you'd prefer?" his assistant asked.

"Just whatever you can arrange. See if you can get appointments with the rest of the board members as well, but slot those three in first." The board members who hadn't yet agreed to vote in a block with him were the first priority. The moment his truce with Ryder was done, he'd be primed to pounce.

"I'll set them up and email you the times. Anything else?"

"Not at the moment, but I'll be in the office in a few hours, and I'll update you then."

"I'll see you soon, Mr. Kentrell," she said, and he disconnected.

He pulled his pants up and zipped them, noticing April sitting on the edge of the bed, dressed. "I thought you had a truce with Ryder?" she said softly.

"Only until we've dealt with JT Hartley." He slid his arms through the sleeves of his shirt and retrieved his cell. "And the second that happens, I'll be ready."

April listened as Seth made call after call, planning, plotting, and turning back into the consummate businessman. And her heart broke into a thousand shards.

He'd asked her to extend her stay, to spend an extra night with him, but hadn't even consulted her when he'd told his assistant he'd be back in the office within the hour. Hadn't even thought to mention he was breaking his invitation when he'd spoken to her. Hot tears pushed at the edges of her eyes but she wouldn't let them fall.

Everything she'd suspected was true—the moment he thought he had what he wanted, he was back to being the Seth she'd met in the hospital. The Seth she'd seen with his half brother yesterday. Oh, she didn't doubt his desire for her was real, was honest, and she hadn't expected they'd sail off into the sunset.

Yet watching his transformation from the man who'd made love to her into the one who couldn't get out of the bed fast enough when he believed he'd won, made her want to curl into a ball.

But it shouldn't hurt so much. Shouldn't cause her world to come crashing down, pinning her crumpled soul to the spot, not when she'd known this was a possibility. Unless…

She loved him.

Stomach in freefall, she squeezed her eyes shut and tried to deny it, but couldn't.

How utterly stupid. She'd fallen in love with the one man she knew she shouldn't. And the feeling obviously wasn't mutual—he'd barely spared her a second thought once he had what he wanted.

Of course, he didn't have any loyalty to his half brother either, already plotting to outmaneuver him. Perhaps Macy was right—their father had really done a number on all the brothers, and Seth wasn't capable of anything more than he'd already shown her.

She stood—not wanting to be on the bed they'd made love in so recently—and searched for her shoes. She had to get out, return to the life she'd remembered.

Alone.

She'd planned to do this by herself, but, knowing she loved him, *alone* now had a whole new level of meaning.

And she needed to consult her legal team about the challenge to her contract for the hotel. She'd fight on, no question. Leave it to the courts to decide, not Seth's lawyers. This hotel was too important.

Seth strode back into the bedroom, phone wedged between shoulder and ear, pulled a suitcase from the cupboard and began to throw clothes in from the drawers and shelves.

Unsure whether to wait or go now, she edged toward the door. Her bags were already packed. The concierge had brought them up earlier, so all she needed to do was have them call her a cab.

Seth finished the call and threw the phone down on the bed beside the suitcase, then rested his hands on his hips and met her gaze. "I have to go."

She found an understanding smile for him as she folded her arms under her breasts. It wasn't his fault she'd fallen in love. "I guessed."

"I'm sorry for rushing off," he said, thrusting his long fingers through his hair. "I asked you to stay the night."

"You have a lot to do now."

He came to her, reached for her hands and interlaced their fingers. "April, this doesn't have to affect us."

She seized the moment, one of their last, drinking him in, creating a memory—of his face, of the intensity in his dark blue eyes—that could sustain her. Then she took a breath, and stepped back, unlacing their fingers. "We're both leaving. Going back to the lives we had before I was in that accident."

He followed her step. "Meet me when you're back in New York. Tomorrow night."

"Seth—"

"I won't give you up, April," he warned with a raised eyebrow. "Not after this morning. We can continue seeing each other there, just as easily as here."

Seeing each other? She looked pointedly at the rumpled bed. "You mean sleeping together."

He cocked his head to the side. "You won't share my bed because I won our tussle for the hotel?"

It sounded childish when he put it like that, but he had to know this was about so much more. He'd told her once that nothing good ever came from love and commitment. What else could he want from her besides a sleeping partner?

Though it hurt to ask, she had to know. "Explain to me what you're looking for in continuing to see me."

"We enjoy each other," he said with a trace of the earlier heat in his eyes.

"Seth, I understand your relationship with Bramson Holdings." How he'd dropped her like a hot potato not ten minutes ago when the company needed him, despite already asking her to stay. How he was planning to keep a man who could be his brother from their father's legacy. "Bramson Holdings is your wife. If we keep seeing each other back in New York, you'd want me as a mistress. Someone you see on the side."

He scowled at her. "That's a hell of a thing to say."

Inside she cringed from his accusation, but the truth

was the only time she'd had one hundred percent of his focus was when she was an obstacle to gaining control of the Bramson Holdings board, or when they were in bed. There had been slivers of time—laughing, holding her hand, kissing—when she could have believed he might feel more for her, but she'd been deluding herself.

So she straightened her spine and didn't hold back. "Tell me you're looking for more than a body to warm your bed when you have spare moments. Someone who understands your priorities are all about the family business. A woman who'll fit around your career. Tell me you want more than that and I'll listen."

Seth's eyes widened. "You're asking for a commitment?"

"No, I'm well aware of how you feel about commitments—'nothing good can come of them,'" she said, paraphrasing his words. "But I won't get involved with someone with a closed heart—start something that has no chance of going anywhere."

"We're long past *starting* something, April," he said, jaw clenched.

And that was precisely the problem—she was already in love with him. She winced as the knowledge lanced a new wound in her heart, but she met his gaze. "Just be straight with me."

"You want to know what I really think?" Every muscle in his body seemed to tense in turn. "People in love are less than themselves. They make bad decisions, do things they know they shouldn't, humiliate themselves. I refuse to be love's fool."

She covered her mouth with her hand, horrified at the depth of his hard-hearted beliefs. "You really believe that?"

"I've seen it firsthand all my life. I watched my mother humiliate herself by accepting my father while he was still married to Ryder's mother. I heard the snide comments people made behind their backs when we went out. I saw men proposition her when my father wasn't around because they thought she was easy." His face paled and his eyes squinted almost shut at the memory. "Jesse had women chasing him for what they could get. He didn't care—he was happy to be used because it was in the name of *love*."

Faced with his anguish, April swayed on her feet—she could feel it radiating from him in waves, a living thing. What chance did he have of happiness in the face of so much pain? "So you'll never commit to someone. Marry?" she whispered. "Have a family?"

Cupping the side of her face with his palm, he pinned her with an angst-ridden gaze. "I can't offer you forever, but we're good together, April. Why not just enjoy what we can have?"

A ball of emotion pressed hard on her throat and she pushed her fingertips against it to try and ease the ache. But nothing could ease the ache in her heart.

She loved him.

He wanted a mistress.

Needing space to think, to breathe, she took another step back, finding the wall behind her. "I think we should go back to our lives. I need to start over, find out who I am. I have decisions about my career to make."

He stepped in, crowding her, eyes serious. "I'll call you when we get back."

There was no purpose in extending this conversation— she placed her palms on his chest and pushed lightly. He moved enough to let her wriggle past, and she slipped on the shoes she'd found. She swallowed hard, wishing it was as easy to find the composure she needed to end this with any kind of dignity.

She straightened slowly. "Please don't call me, Seth."

A procession of emotions crossed his face, each replaced by the next before she could identify them. Then he pulled her into a fierce hug. "I refuse to believe this is goodbye," he said over her head.

After several heartbeats, she turned to rest her cheek against his shoulder. "You have a company to win from one brother and another potential brother to deal with. I have to decide what I want from my career, and possibly go through my mother to get there. Then pick up all the pieces of my life that I've let go while I've been here. And I'll be pressing on with my claim for this hotel, regardless of your legal team's opinion. We'll both be far too busy for anything else."

He tugged her face up and kissed her roughly, claiming her mouth, and she wrapped her arms behind his neck, pulling him closer, wanting everything he had to give in this, their last kiss.

Then she drew back. "I have to go." He didn't release her. "Seth, I have to go, and so do you. You're expected back at your office in a few hours."

"I'll get the concierge to take your bags to my car."

"No," she said, voice breaking.

He drew in a controlled breath through stiff lips. "We're both going back down to the city. I'll drive you."

"Seth, let's just say goodbye here. Please." She'd already said goodbye to him too many times—yesterday at the lighthouse, this morning in her bed, and now again, here in his suite. She simply wouldn't survive another parting.

He must have read something of her desperation. His face closed down and he dropped his arms to his sides. "Let me call you a car."

Grateful, she nodded. If she had to tell someone over the

phone to order a cab to leave this place, leave Seth, she'd probably burst into tears.

He picked up the handset of the hotel phone and pressed a button. "Good afternoon, Anna, this is Seth Kentrell. Please book a limo to New York, to leave as soon as possible. Charge it to my account."

Seth watched April as he hung up the phone, his stomach in knots. "They said they should be able to have one here within the hour."

She frowned. "You didn't have to pay for my trip."

"It's done," he grated. "I'll have the piano shipped as soon as you're settled. Let me know."

Her eyes squeezed shut for the briefest of seconds. "Leave it here, in the ballroom. It belongs at this hotel."

Damn it! She wanted to refuse that, too? He rubbed a hand over the tense muscles at the back of his neck. She wouldn't take the piano, or a ride back to the city. *Or him.* "It belongs with you."

"You forget that I still intend to claim this hotel. But regardless of who ends up with ownership, I'd like to think of the piano still here," she said, voice thick, "being played by other pianists, enjoyed by audiences of hotel guests, the way it was when my father was here." Her eyes met his with a wistful sadness. "I'm not going to accept the piano, Seth. But I will accept the ride. Thank you."

His gaze locked on hers but he didn't reply. Couldn't find the words to say her decisions were fine with him, because they weren't. *It was all wrong.* And even if he had the words, his throat was so tight, he wouldn't have got them out.

"If you don't mind," April said, looking down at her shoes, "I'll wait for the car down by the ocean. I'll miss that view."

He nodded and she came over and pressed a kiss to his cheek. "Thank you, Seth. For everything."

And then she was gone and the room was empty. He stood, arms at his sides, confused. He'd won. The hotel was safe, and he could move, full steam ahead. So why did he feel as if he'd lost?

Three weeks later, Seth sat in his penthouse apartment, looking out at the night sky and the iridescent moon that had risen high. He ached for April, wanted to talk to her about tonight's stars, see what she knew about them. He rattled the ice in the Scotch, then threw it down his throat and plunked the glass on the table beside his armchair. His eyes roamed the room and he wished there was an interconnecting door to lead him directly to April. He could almost hear the faint strains of her piano on the breeze.

Would she ever visit the Lighthouse Hotel after she lost her unwinnable case? It'd be a damn shame if she didn't. The heart of the place would always belong to her.

And then it hit him, why he felt like he'd lost the battle since she'd walked out the door of his suite twenty-two days ago. The hotel should have been April's. It meant too much to her to take it away.

A vision of her at the top of the lighthouse—eyes shining with appreciation of the view—filled his mind. A slash of pain tore through his chest, and he pounded a fist on his breastbone to dislodge it. Then an image of her sitting on the grass near the water, her legs tucked up under her skirt, hair blowing in the breeze. Then, in his arms, looking at the stars above. Underneath him on the piano. Watching the video of her father. Walking along the dock to meet him. Opening the interconnecting door to her suite, rumpled from sleep. Regaining her memory... He squeezed his eyes shut, trying to block out the visions, but that only made them more vivid.

Breath coming too fast, he strode to the kitchen and poured another Scotch. What was this pull she had over him? Was this *love*—the insatiable need to be with her, to have her in his bed, to listen to her talk, make her happy?

Regardless of its label, he was having none of it. His mother had often told him that "true love is worth any sacrifice," but she'd been dead wrong. Giving someone any measure of control over yourself was more than a sacrifice—it was dangerous and demeaning. Nothing good could come of it, only opportunities for pain, humiliation and becoming a fool for a woman.

He downed the drink and discarded the glass, wishing the burn on his throat was stronger, to wipe out every other thought and emotion.

If *this* was love, he wanted no part of it.

But—he pressed his fingers to his throbbing temples— there was one thing that needed to be done. He knew it bone deep.

Palms damp, he reached into his pocket for his cell, dialed Angus Jackson's number, and for the first time in his life, he did something without caring about the repercussions on his career. He bought the Lighthouse Hotel from Bramson Holdings from his personal funds and arranged to have it signed over into April's name.

Seemed he was making a fool of himself over a woman after all. He'd never see her again, but he was giving her his hotel.

Twelve

April looked in the illuminated mirror and surveyed the makeup artist's and hair stylist's work. It would look good onstage tonight, under the spotlights—dramatic up close, yet soft and romantic from a distance.

"Thanks, Sharon, Jody," she said to the team with genuine warmth. These women had been making her look the part since long before her accident, but they had new jobs to go to starting tomorrow. They wished her well as she slipped through the door.

There was under an hour left till she was due onstage. She'd done the sound check, had spoken to the backup band and finished in hair and makeup. The last thing to do was dress in her costume—a silver-sequined sheath that reminded her of the stars twinkling at night—and do her vocal warm-ups with the keyboard in her room.

She headed down the corridor, catching a glimpse of a promo poster for tonight's performance. It had been billed as her "farewell" concert, but she planned to do more, just nothing in the foreseeable future. Perhaps in a few years she'd reconsider. Almost six weeks had passed since she'd left the Lighthouse Hotel behind. And Seth. And her heart hadn't healed. Sure, it had developed scars, so the pain wasn't quite as fresh; but when she was all alone she yearned for him so much she didn't think she'd ever be whole again.

Her legal team had agreed with Seth's—that there was no point asking a court to validate the contract signed with Jesse. She'd told them to go ahead anyway, but she had next to no optimism about the outcome.

She pushed open the door to her private dressing room, needing the space alone to center herself. On her dressing table was a letter, addressed to her, care of her new agent. The handwriting on the front reminded her of Seth's and that made her smile. *Everything* reminded her of Seth—yachts, the moon in the sky, blueberry muffins, lighthouses, New England, the business section of the paper, pianos.

Especially pianos—shiny, black baby grands.

There was one waiting for her onstage, and she knew she'd created a challenge for herself tonight—to keep her mind on the concert and not let it drift to Seth leaning her back on a similar model, then prowling over her, taking her. Owning her. A prickling heat slithered across her skin and she laid a hand over her heart, as if that could tame the hurtling beat. She was appearing onstage in forty minutes—not the time to be distracted by her longing for the man she loved, body, heart and soul.

She picked up the envelope and slit it open. A letter fell out and a thicker packet of folded papers. She opened the letter first.

Dear April,
I've enclosed the deed to the Lighthouse Hotel. It already belonged to you in spirit; I should have seen that sooner. Now it belongs to you completely.
S

April swayed then fell back into a chair as her knees buckled. She read the words again, trying to force her mind to process the note's meaning. Then she picked up the deed and read every word on that. *It was true.* She pinched the bridge of her nose, holding back the tears that would ruin the makeup that had just been meticulously applied.

That sweet, foolish man—he'd given her his *hotel*.

Seth slid into his seat in the rear of the darkened theater, his gut clenched tight as though he was about to jump from a plane. April's beautiful voice filled the hall, touching his soul. Touching his heart. *Torture.*

The concert was nearing its end. When he'd bought his ticket, he wasn't sure if he'd attend. He'd even made other plans for tonight. But like an addict getting his fix, he'd ended up here anyway.

His breathing was irregular as he looked down on the stage—April sat at her piano so far below, but large screens on either side of the stage showed close-ups. She was spectacular—hair shining like strands of gold and bronze under the lights, smile wide and engaging as she sang the Louis Armstrong tune he'd seen her play on the video as a thirteen-year-old. Her dress reminded him of a galaxy of stars that sparkled almost as brightly as her eyes.

He strained forward in the seat, blood storming through his veins, aching to be closer, to touch her. Which was precisely the reason nothing would ever happen between them again. And why it'd been a blessing in disguise when she'd turned down his offer to keep seeing him when she moved back to New York.

He felt too damn much for her.

He completely understood why his mother had let his father make a fool of her for years—if he and April were together, she'd have him wrapped around her finger in no time, and he'd wind up not being *him*. He'd be a weakened version of himself, one without complete control over his own actions, open to making bad decisions.

He might have given her the hotel, but he wasn't sticking around to be her fool.

And what if she ever left him? Nausea roiled in his stomach just thinking about it. It simply wasn't a situation he was prepared to put himself in.

He'd take this last hit of his addiction, and then go cold turkey. Afterward, he'd find a nice, uncomplicated relationship, where the woman didn't make him feel too much, where she stayed in the mental compartment he assigned for relationships, and couldn't blend into all aspects of his life.

Where she wouldn't be April.

The song ended and the audience around him erupted. Smiling in acknowledgment of the applause, she stood, took a microphone from a stand and came to the edge of the stage.

"Thank you," she said several times. When the din died down a little, she went on. "I need to introduce you to the best backup musicians in the business." Another roar went up from the crowd, and April individually named each of the people who'd played with her.

After waiting for silence, she spoke again. "I'd like to finish with a different song than the one we had planned." She turned to her musicians, who looked at her expectantly. "It's new—I haven't even shared it with my band yet, so you'll have to put up with just my piano accompaniment."

The audience clapped as the musicians behind her all lowered their instruments and waited like everyone else.

Seth began to rise. He'd seen enough to appease his morbid curiosity. Too much. He needed to get out.

"I wrote this song for someone who helped me once. When I was vulnerable and facing my greatest challenge, someone stepped up to the plate and gave me the shelter and support I needed. This is for him."

Seth froze, heart in his mouth. Could she mean…?

He sank back into his seat.

April returned the microphone to its stand, sat back at the baby grand and played a few introductory notes. Then he heard his name. It was whisper-quiet since the microphone was no longer close, and most people would have missed it, but there was no doubt in his mind.

Seth broke out in a cold sweat. She'd written a song for him. Was playing it for thousands of strangers. Was exposing herself for no good reason. What was she thinking?

April began to sing, and the haunting melody rose into the room, curling around his heart.

The other people disappeared from his vision, the distance between them shrank, and it was just the two of them in all the world. Her voice filled the auditorium, and it was beautiful, so much more than he deserved. Without realizing it, he was on his feet and out the door.

Drawing on her last reserves of energy, April sang the ending of the new song, and as the final note faded away, the audience gradually stood and broke into loud applause. Her backup band clapped, too, with honest appreciation.

This, its first performance, had ripped her chest open and exposed her fractured heart to the world. Surely it would never be as hard to sing as tonight?

It was a good song, she could feel it in her bones, and knew it would become a single. Unfortunately, that meant she'd set herself up for requests to sing about Seth whenever she chose to perform in the future, stopping her pain from healing.

If she'd had any doubts about the strength of the song, then the reaction of the people in the auditorium had just erased them. The applause was still going. She appreciated it, but truth was, she was emotionally overwrought after that finale. It was a song straight from her heart, and singing it had taken every drop of emotion she had inside her and squeezed tight. She had nothing left. If there hadn't been thousands of people watching, she would have slumped into a ball and slept for a year. Actually, she might just do that when she got home.

She bowed, and the musicians behind her took up their instruments again, playing the exit music as she left the stage. She gave a wave to the people who'd paid to see her perform tonight and escaped into the wings. Her mother—whom she had a fledgling attempt at a fresh relationship with—her agent and Emerson were all waiting just offstage. Too exhausted for anything complicated, she headed for Emerson, who wrapped her in a bear hug. "Congratulations, sweetie."

She hugged him back, appreciating his support, but Emerson's arms weren't the arms she ached to have embracing her. After singing about Seth, she was too raw, too fragile to cope with all the well-wishers who were crowding around. Her pulse still raced, and if anyone asked her who the song was about, she was liable to burst into tears.

She leaned up and whispered into Emerson's ear, "I need

to get out of here. Can you get me back to my dressing room?"

An enigmatic smile stretched across his face before he nodded and turned, keeping her tucked tightly to his side.

Within minutes they'd broken free from the throng, Emerson clearing the way with his booming voice and an outstretched arm. When they reached the door to her dressing room, Emerson turned her to face him and kissed the top of her head. "You did well tonight, kid."

She looked up at him, surprised. When he attended one of her concerts he usually came in with her afterward to share a bottle of Champagne. Perhaps he'd understood from her body language that she needed to be alone.

She took a step back to see him more clearly. "You're not coming in?"

"Not this time," he said, grinning. Holding her elbow, he turned her, opened the door and pushed her through before quickly shutting it behind her.

She blinked. The room was overflowing with roses, lilies, gerbera daisies and balloons. That often happened after a concert—fans and friends sent flowers and gifts, like chocolates to be placed in her room during the performance. What didn't normally arrive while she was onstage was a man.

She blinked and blinked again but Seth was still there, standing across the room, motionless as he watched her, his face taut. Her heart tripped, missing beats, hammering too fast against her ribs. The magnetic pull of him was almost too strong to resist, but unable to read his expression, she stayed rooted to the spot.

"Hello," she finally managed.

"Hello," he rasped, then cleared his throat. "I saw some of the concert."

His eyes burned with intensity, but his face was so closed, so contained, that she couldn't identify what emotion it was that his gaze held. Her chest filled with a hoard of butterflies. Had he heard the new song? He was such a private man that even though she hadn't named him, he might be offended that she'd spoken publicly about their time together and her feelings.

Throat parched, she reached for the glass of water that always awaited her and drank deeply. Then she looked at him over the rim. "Did you like the concert?" she asked tentatively.

He nodded, but his feet stayed firmly in place. "I heard the new song, too."

Her stomach somersaulted. "Do you mind?" She nibbled her bottom lip. "I know I should have checked with you first—"

"I didn't mind," he said, still not moving or showing which emotion he was feeling so vividly.

She breathed out a relieved breath but couldn't relax— not with her body screaming for him. And not while she didn't know why he was here. She glanced around the room and saw the deed to the hotel still sitting on a table, surrounded by bunches of carnations. Her heart squeezed tight as it had when she'd opened the envelope. "You gave me a hotel," she blurted.

"Yes." He shifted his weight to the other leg.

It was the most staggering thing anyone had ever done for her, and even though she couldn't take it, she'd treasure the gesture forever, adding it to the precious memories of their time in Queensport.

She crossed to the table and picked up the deed, took one last look and passed it to him with trembling fingers. "I can't accept it."

He didn't make a move to take it from her, and his forehead puckered into a frown. "Of course you can."

Her hand dropped to her side as she considered how best to refuse his gift. Giving back a huge asset like the Lighthouse Hotel was hardly like giving back a pair of earrings. And he'd need it—he spent all their time together trying to get it back because it was so important to his career. Which was the perfect point to convince him.

"Won't this affect your place on the board?"

"No." He shrugged one shoulder casually, belying the rigidity of his stance.

"No? But when I signed that contract with Jesse, you were so desperate to get it back."

"Because the contract you had with Jesse meant our income from the sale was far below the market valuation. This time Bramson Holdings sold it to me for a fair price. There's a difference. The ramifications are nothing I can't deal with. I'll still win over the board, no question."

He was serious. Her mouth opened and closed twice before she could get her voice to work. "You *personally* bought me an entire hotel?"

Seeming uncomfortable with her reaction, he waved her concern away with a flick of his wrist—the most movement he'd made since she entered the room.

The deed fell from her hand to the floor and she swooped to pick it up and laid it back on the table. "It must have cost you a fortune," she said, unable to keep the awe from her voice.

His gaze didn't falter. "It was the right thing to do."

She'd known from the start that Seth Kentrell was a man who always did what he considered the right thing. But this was too much. "Thank you," she said, "but I still can't take it. Besides, I don't need it—I've made some changes to my career and I'm stepping back from performing even without the hotel. It was the thing that started me thinking I could really step back, especially with the connection to my father, but I'll find another way."

He looked as if he wanted to step closer but restrained himself. "You were wonderful out there. I know you spoke about giving up your music career the day your memory returned, but seeing you perform onstage—"

"Not give it up entirely." She'd given the decision a lot of thought both before the accident and since her memory had returned. It was what she needed to do. "I won't be a full-time performer, touring and recording. I'll find something else that gives my heart wings."

His eyes narrowed, seizing on the point. "Like the Lighthouse Hotel does."

"Like that," she acknowledged. "But the hotel belongs to you and your family."

He reached to run a fingertip across the petals of a pale pink rose beside him, before glancing up and meeting her eyes again. "Will you tell me something personal if I ask?"

She couldn't imagine denying him much of anything, but that was a secret she needed to guard closely—he already had the advantage, just by virtue of her love for him. She reached for the water jug and refilled her glass. "I'll try."

"There was a line...." He paused and his Adam's apple bobbed down then up.

She had a feeling she knew just which line. She sipped her water and waited for him to expose her soul.

"About your heart belonging under the stars...." he trailed off.

"With you," she whispered.

Face still guarded, he nodded. "You loved me back then?"

The air leached from her lungs. There was no way to

avoid this, to deny and plead the fifth. Not when she'd written her feelings into the lyrics. Her eyes drifted shut for a long moment, then she opened them and faced him. "Yes."

"And you're willing to tell the world," he said, voice strained.

She carefully set the glass on her table before her jittery fingers lost their grip. What was he thinking? She still couldn't read his face and it was driving her crazy. "I needed to be honest, to not censor it, for the song to work."

His chest expanded, held, then slowly returned to normal. "It was the bravest thing I've ever seen in my life." His navy blue eyes burned into hers.

"Brave?" She gulped the word more than said it.

"People will figure out the song was for me. Enough people saw us together at the hotel to put two and two together. And you told them you love me."

"I'm sorry," she said, confused about his meaning and where this was going.

He took a step closer. "Don't apologize. I watched my mother spend her life being publicly humiliated by my father." His jaw clenched and unclenched. "He'd say the words of love to her and us, but then he'd go home on weekends, or when it suited him, to his wife and Ryder."

She remembered him saying on the yacht that he'd watch his mother cry at those times, and her heart wanted to weep for him. "Your father was insensitive and cruel."

His head tilted in agreement. "She told me love was worth it, but I thought she was wrong. *Nothing* was worth that sort of pain." Eyes bleak, he drove his fingers through his dark hair, leaving it rumpled. "I've steered away from ever letting another person have control over me."

The final pieces of the jigsaw puzzle that explained his

guarded heart fell into place, and she ached to hold him and ease the old pain that still bound him. "I can understand why," she said instead.

He took another step closer, to within touching distance. "At the hotel, in those days we spent together, I started to have feelings for you, but I didn't want them—they're dangerous."

"Yes," she whispered. She remembered watching the struggle he'd waged within himself, the inner torment that had followed whenever desire had flared in his eyes.

"And when you refused to see me back here in the city, I realized they were more than simple feelings." His hand lifted to cup the side of her face, sending Champagne fizz through her bloodstream, his thumb gently stroking. "Which only made me more determined to smother them."

Smother them? If he wasn't so serious, she'd want to laugh at his view of his actions. "But you bought me a hotel," she pointed out.

"As I said, that was the right thing to do." He reached and took both her hands, looking down at their intertwined fingers. "But it didn't mean I could trust myself around you."

Her hands in his felt so *right* that she took a moment to simply absorb the sensation. The slide of his palm against hers, the heat that permeated through to her fingers. All too soon, it was no longer enough, so she prompted him, "Then why did you come tonight?"

"I couldn't resist the chance to see you perform." A rueful smile curved his mouth. "It was safe—you wouldn't know I was here, and there were thousands of people in the room with us, but I could see you again."

The thought of him in the audience tonight, wanting to

see her as much as she'd been wanting to see him, made her skin quiver. "And yet you came backstage?"

"It was that song," he said slowly. "It undid me."

She moistened her lips and watched him watch the movement.

"Seeing you expose yourself like that, wear your heart on your sleeve, knowing that people may figure it out, was a revelation." He shook his head, as if still surprised.

"It wasn't easy," she admitted. She'd been totally wrung out when she finished singing. And part of her had been braced ever since she'd written it, knowing Seth would hear it sooner or later. It had turned out to be much sooner than she'd expected. And she still wasn't sure if that was a good or a bad thing.

Eyes filled with admiration, he lifted their joined hands to nudge her chin higher. "But you found the courage and did it. Which made me realize that I needed to do the same."

The room swam as she mentally replayed his words. *I needed to do the same.* "W-what are you saying?"

"I love you, April Fairchild, and I don't care who knows it. I don't care if it makes me a fool, and I don't care how the media and public react. All that's important is how *you* feel." His gaze zoomed in on her as he waited.

Tears stung at the back of her nose, clogging her throat. They were the words she'd dreamed of this man saying, and part of her wondered if she'd heard him right or if her imagination was giving her what she wanted most. "Love… me…?"

Eyes fierce, he gripped her hands more tightly. "I promise you that if you give your heart to me, it will always be safe. I'll treasure it and protect it above everything."

She wound her arms around his neck, wanting to show

him what words couldn't express, and he groaned, pulling her flush along his body. She expected fervor, intensity, yet he kept the kiss sweet, brushing his lips gently along hers. Her knees buckled and she swayed, and he held her steady with an arm around her waist as he tenderly kissed the corners of her mouth. But she wanted him *so* much…. She parted her lips and stroked her tongue into the depths of his mouth, connecting with him, uniting with him on every level. It was everything. *He* was everything.

He leaned his forehead against hers. "Is that an *I love you, too,* kiss or an *I'm letting you down easy* kiss?"

She smiled and arched an eyebrow. "It's an *I love you more than any woman's ever loved a man* kiss."

"My favorite kind," he growled as he pulled her tight again. "Do you have any more of them?"

Melting into him, she lifted her face. His lips were hungrier this time, demanding, and she gave and took in equal measure, until he wrenched his mouth away, panting. Wrapped in his arms, she stood in a golden-hued silence for endless moments as they both caught their breath. It wasn't the end of a kiss, it was the start of something bigger. Better. Happiness bubbled up inside her chest.

"Where do we go from here?" she asked.

He took a deep breath and let it out slowly. "I'm not sure. I've never done this before. But I think we start by leaving this building and going back to my apartment. Then at some stage after that, we get married." A lazy smile spread across his face. "And then we spend our lives together, being happier than we could have dreamed."

She could believe that—if they were together then happiness was inevitable. "Seth, I want you to know your heart will be safe with me, too. I'll look after it like the treasure it is."

"I know you will." He wrapped an arm around her shoulders and she leaned into him as they headed for the door, toward the rest of their lives.

Epilogue

April felt for the next concrete step up, using only her feet, since her eyes were covered by the hands of the man standing directly behind her.

"One more, and we're there," Seth said, his voice low and husky near her ear.

She took the final step and his hands dropped to her waist. As always, her heart soared as she looked out at the lighthouse's spectacular view of the ocean and night sky. She'd never get enough of this place. Or the man with her. Sighing contentedly, she leaned back into him.

Then she noticed the huge telescope set up a little farther along, almost around the bend of the curving, glassed-in platform. "Oh," she gasped, and rushed over for a closer look.

She ran a hand down the outside. She had a telescope at home, but this was bigger, more powerful. And being in Queensport, up in an unused lighthouse, she'd see farther than when she was in the city, where the lights and smog interfered with visibility.

"Oh, Seth," she breathed as she looked at one of the shiny chrome controls.

He moved up behind her again. "Any star girl worth her salt needs a telescope in her own hotel."

She arched an eyebrow as she turned back to face him. "*Our* hotel."

"I signed it over to you." He smiled indulgently and placed a kiss at the corner of her mouth.

They'd had this discussion several times in the weeks since her concert, but she wasn't budging on this point. "I'm having that changed to include both our names. It's a symbol of our relationship. Strong. Permanent. Ours."

"I think it's more a symbol of you. Stunning. Resilient. Mine." A reluctant grin spread across his face. "I guess I just proved your argument."

Her grin matched his. "You did. It's *ours*."

He silenced further conversation by claiming her mouth, and she moaned as she accepted the kiss, wanting more. Always wanting more.

When the kiss ended, he leaned his forehead against hers, his breathing heavy. "Ours," he agreed.

* * * * *

COMING NEXT MONTH

Available March 8, 2011

REQUEST YOUR FREE BOOKS!

2 FREE NOVELS
PLUS 2
FREE GIFTS!

Silhouette®

Desire®

Passionate, Powerful, Provocative!

YES! Please send me 2 FREE Silhouette Desire® novels and my 2 FREE gifts (gifts are worth about $10). After receiving them, if I don't wish to receive any more books, I can return the shipping statement marked "cancel." If I don't cancel, I will receive 6 brand-new novels every month and be billed just $4.05 per book in the U.S. or $4.74 per book in Canada. That's a saving of at least 15% off the cover price! It's quite a bargain! Shipping and handling is just 50¢ per book in the U.S. and 75¢ per book in Canada.* I understand that accepting the 2 free books and gifts places me under no obligation to buy anything. I can always return a shipment and cancel at any time. Even if I never buy another book, the two free books and gifts are mine to keep forever.

225/326 SDN FC65

Name   (PLEASE PRINT)

Address   Apt. #

City   State/Prov.   Zip/Postal Code

Signature (if under 18, a parent or guardian must sign)

Mail to the **Reader Service:**

IN U.S.A.: P.O. Box 1867, Buffalo, NY 14240-1867
IN CANADA: P.O. Box 609, Fort Erie, Ontario L2A 5X3

Not valid for current subscribers to Silhouette Desire books.

Want to try two free books from another line?
Call 1-800-873-8635 or visit www.ReaderService.com.

* Terms and prices subject to change without notice. Prices do not include applicable taxes. Sales tax applicable in N.Y. Canadian residents will be charged applicable taxes. Offer not valid in Quebec. This offer is limited to one order per household. All orders subject to credit approval. Credit or debit balances in a customer's account(s) may be offset by any other outstanding balance owed by or to the customer. Please allow 4 to 6 weeks for delivery. Offer available while quantities last.

Your Privacy—The Reader Service is committed to protecting your privacy. Our Privacy Policy is available online at www.ReaderService.com or upon request from the Reader Service.

We make a portion of our mailing list available to reputable third parties that offer products we believe may interest you. If you prefer that we not exchange your name with third parties, or if you wish to clarify or modify your communication preferences, please visit us at www.ReaderService.com/consumerschoice or write to us at Reader Service Preference Service, P.O. Box 9062, Buffalo, NY 14269. Include your complete name and address.

USA TODAY *bestselling author Lynne Graham*
is back with a thrilling new trilogy
SECRETLY PREGNANT, CONVENIENTLY WED

Three heroines must marry alpha males to keep
their dreams…but Alejandro, Angelo and Cesario
are not about to be tamed!

Book 1—JEMIMA'S SECRET
Available March 2011 from Harlequin Presents®.

JEMIMA yanked open a drawer in the sideboard to find Alfie's birth certificate. Her son was her husband's child. It was a question of telling the truth whether she liked it or not. She extended the certificate to Alejandro.

"This has to be nonsense," Alejandro asserted.

"Well, if you can find some other way of explaining how I managed to give birth by that date and Alfie not be yours, I'd like to hear it," Jemima challenged.

Alejandro glanced up, golden eyes bright as blades and as dangerous. "All this proves is that you must still have been pregnant when you walked out on our marriage. It does not automatically follow that the child is mine."

"'I know it doesn't suit you to hear this news now and I really didn't want to tell you. But I can't lie to you about it. Someday Alfie may want to look you up and get acquainted."

"If what you have just told me is the truth, if that little boy does prove to be mine, it was vindictive and extremely selfish of you to leave me in ignorance!"

Jemima paled. "When I left you, I had no idea that I was still pregnant."

"Two years is a long period of time, yet you made no attempt to inform me that I might be a father. I will want DNA tests to confirm your claim before I make any decision about what I want to do."

"Do as you like," she told him curtly. "*I* know who Alfie's father is and there has never been any doubt of his identity."

"I will make arrangements for the tests to be carried out and I will see you again when the result is available," Alejandro drawled with lashings of dark Spanish masculine reserve.

"I'll contact a solicitor and start the divorce," Jemima proffered in turn.

Alejandro's eyes narrowed in a piercing scrutiny that made her uncomfortable. "It would be foolish to do anything before we have that DNA result."

"I disagree," Jemima flashed back. "I should have applied for a divorce the minute I left you!"

Alejandro quirked an ebony brow. "And why didn't you?"

Jemima dealt him a fulminating glance but said nothing, merely moving past him to open her front door in a blunt invitation for him to leave.

"I'll be in touch," he delivered on the doorstep.

What is Alejandro's next move? Perhaps rekindling their marriage is the only solution! But will Jemima agree?

Find out in Lynne Graham's
exciting new romance
JEMIMA'S SECRET

Available March 2011
from Harlequin Presents®.

Start your Best Body today with these top 3 nutrition tips!

1. **SHOP THE PERIMETER OF THE GROCERY STORE:** The good stuff—fruits, veggies, lean proteins and dairy—always line the outer edges of the store. When you veer into the center aisles, you enter the temptation zone, where the unhealthy foods live.

2. **WATCH PORTION SIZES:** Most portion sizes in restaurants are nearly twice the size of a true serving and at home, it's easy to "clean your plate." Use these easy serving guidelines:
   - Protein: the palm of your hand
   - Grains or Fruit: a cup of your hand
   - Veggies: the palm of two open hands

3. **USE THE RAINBOW RULE FOR PRODUCE:** Your produce drawers should be filled with every color of fruits and vegetables. The greater the variety, the more vitamins and other nutrients you add to your diet.

Find these and many more helpful tips in

YOUR BEST BODY NOW
by
TOSCA RENO
WITH STACY BAKER

Bestselling Author of
THE EAT-CLEAN DIET®

Available wherever books are sold!